THE SINGLE LIFE

THE SINGLE LIFE

MARQUITA B.

Corks and Coils Publishing

ISBN: (Ebook) 978-1-7330183-7-1
ISBN: (Paperback) 978-1-7330183-3-3
ISBN: (Hardcover) 978-1-7330183-6-4

This is a work of fiction. Any references or similarities to actual events, real people, living or dead or to real locales are used to give a sense of reality. Any similarity in other names, characters, places and incidents is entirely coincidental.

Library of Congress Control Number: 2020921389
First printing edition 2020

Dedicated to my amazing husband and daughter.

I Love You Both!

INTRODUCTION

I took one last sip of wine before rising from my sofa, rinsing out the glass, and heading to my bedroom. It had been a lazy Sunday evening of sipping wine and watching TV, and in the midst of my *me time*, I'd intentionally ignored the fact that I had an early morning train to catch. The red numbers from my digital clock glared, unwilling to let me forget. At 11:55, I regretted not taking my butt to bed sooner.

After I finished packing, I showered, wrapped my hair, and jumped onto my California King bed to squeeze in as much sleep as possible before 5 AM. I loved my bed. It was my place of peace and comfort after a long, busy day at work, but most of all, it was all mine.

As I drifted off, I thought about how much I had begun to enjoy the single life.

A few months prior, my ex-husband, Kyle and I, had finalized our divorce after only a few years of marriage. However, that short period of time was enough to hit my life like a whirlwind. So, for the first time in a long time, I had found the calm after the storm I so desperately needed.

I'd only known Kyle for a few months before we got married, but aside from the certificate, you wouldn't even have *known* I was married.

In fact, during the entirety of our barely three-year marriage, Kyle and I were only physically together for about a year. Unfortunately, I had made the mistake of tying the knot with a man I knew absolutely nothing about, and I paid the consequences for my haste to get hitched with a loss of my precious time and a baby that I was too stressed to successfully carry to term. It was just a very painful and challenging time in my life, which is one of the reasons I decided to move. I wanted to get away from anything that reminded me of that pain. So, as I lay in bed reflecting on the past, I basked in the freedom that existed in a space of my own. However, I wasn't always alone.

After my divorce, I had been on a few dates that turned into a few nightcaps, but I always made it clear that I wasn't looking for anything serious. I was in no rush to be tied down to another man. My sex life was great and the men I dated were fine, yet I still relished in the comfort I got from going home alone to a bed I didn't have to share.

I'm not going to lie, getting over Kyle and learning to be comfortable alone took some time and adjusting to, but ultimately, I was able to put Kyle completely in the rearview. Since I'd been single, I started to put myself and my happiness first and live carefree. I was making good money as a contract attorney. I was finally beginning to enjoy my new life: the single life. It allowed me to travel, meet great people, and do whatever the hell I wanted *when* I wanted. Life was good and I was on a high that nothing could bring me down from.

CHAPTER 1

MID-SUMMER, 2003

"Hey, girl. What's up?" I'd just arrived at my hotel room in Manhattan for a three-day legal conference when Toni called. I had some time to spare before I headed downstairs to the first session, so I kicked off my heels and sat on the bed to chat for a bit.

"Hey, girl. What was the name of that drink I loved when we stayed at The Ritz in Paris?" asked Toni.

"Hmmm ... Serendipity?"

"Yeah, that's it! Serendipity! That drink was *so* good. I'm going to see if they can make it for me at the bar near my job. I'm heading to happy hour after work with some of my co-workers, and I've been craving it ever since we left Paris."

"Girl, you better not order that drink on a work night. Those Serendipity's had you twisted, and you know you have a problem with knowing your limits."

I hated to say it, but Toni was a lush. She'd also been known to lose all her inhibitions when drunk and I worried that one day she would end up drunk around people who wouldn't have her back the way I would.

"Girl, cut it out. I'll be fine. I'm just going for a few drinks with some of my colleagues from the office, and then I'm heading home." I could picture the pout I knew was forming on Toni's lips. She hated when I played big sister, especially since she's older than me. "I'm a big girl, Kia. You don't have to worry about me," Toni insisted.

I wasn't convinced, but I decided to let it go. "Okay, girl. Well, don't drink too much and be careful."

"Okay, *Mom*," Toni mocked.

I could picture her rolling her eyes, but I've always been overprotective of the people I love.

"Anyway, what are you up to?"

"Nothing much. I'm here in Manhattan for that conference I told you about last week. I literally just walked into my room when you called me. I need to unpack and freshen up before I head down to the conference in a little bit."

"Oh, I love it in New York! I wish my cheap ass job would sponsor a few conferences for me, but that would never happen. I really need to get a new gig."

"Girl, you're not going anywhere. You've been saying you're going to leave that company for years, but I guarantee you that fat-ass paycheck you're getting is what's making you stay right where you are!" We both laughed.

"Yeah, you're right. They don't sponsor shit, but they do pay good. Anyway, enough about work. Have you seen any good-looking men, yet?"

"Toni, I just got here, on top of that, I am not here for none of that. I'm here for work purposes only."

"Yeah, I bet. Well, what about at home? How's it been living so close to your former side-boo? You know, the one you waited forever to tell me about? What's his name? David?"

"I wouldn't know. I've only seen him a few times since I moved in, and I've only said hi and bye."

"Chile, I don't know how you do it. I could never be just friendly with someone I almost got down and dirty with." I could imagine Toni rolling her eyes through the phone.

I half-listened as Toni went on about how I should give David a chance, even if it was only as friends with benefits. I began to think about how good of a friend David was to me while Kyle was in prison. Bumping into him at my new place was definitely a surprise. After finalizing my divorce with Kyle, I decided I needed an upgrade to my lifestyle, so I moved to a beautiful upscale gated townhouse community. It just so happened, David, an almost-fling of mine, lived a few doors down from me. Now, what are the odds of that happening? Well, in my crazy-ass life, I guess the odds are pretty good. Anyway, while David was still sexy as hell, I still hadn't gotten over a fight he got into with my ex, Kyle, during a funeral of all places. Long story short, Kyle's cousin died, and David just so happened to be an acquaintance of the deceased and was present at the funeral. Now *that* was a shock, but it seems like everyone knows everyone in the DMV.

"Hellooooo ... Kia, are you there?" Toni's voice interrupted my thoughts.

"Yes, girl. I'm sorry. I'm here."

"Well, I was going to wait for a little while, but I have something to tell you ... and I can't hold it in anymore." I could tell Toni was trying to contain her excitement.

"Now you know you can't keep a secret. Girl, what's up?"

"Well, you know how I told you AJ has been acting weird lately, and I was starting to think he wasn't interested in me anymore?"

"Wait, before you go on—do I need to drive down there and beat someone's ass? You know I fight men, right?" I said jokingly.

"No, crazy. You don't have to fight anyone. This is actually good news for me for once in the romance department."

"Okay, girl. So, what is it? You got me over here all anxious...."

"AJ proposed ... and I said yes!"

"Ahhhhhh!!! Are you serious, Toni? Are you really about to be a married woman?"

"Yes, girl! Can you believe it? All this time I thought he was being distant because he was losing interest in me and the whole time, he was just nervous about proposing. So, anyway, you know my wedding is going to be bomb, right? And of course, I want you to be my maid of honor!"

"Oh, Toni! Of course, I'll be your maid of honor. I'm so happy for you! Even though I've never met AJ, if you love him, I'm sure I'll love him too.

I couldn't lie; I was a little worried. Not only was I having flashbacks to my own hasty, failed marriage, but I also couldn't deny the sharp feeling in my gut that something was up with AJ. It was nothing I could put my finger on, but everything Toni told me about AJ seemed too good to be true. He didn't have any kids, had perfect credit, owned a business, had never been married and even owned his own home. The cherry on top was that he had no criminal record. I didn't want to be a Debbie Downer, so I never said anything, but things seemed too perfect with Mr.

AJ, and I had already learned the hard way—perfect men don't exist.

While Toni talked about the type of wedding she wanted to have, I thought about my own marriage. When Kyle and I got married, everything happened so quickly. It was only about a week after we were engaged that we rushed to get married at the courthouse. My own parents weren't at my wedding, that's how rushed it was. Then, a week or so later, Kyle was gone to what I *thought* was Air Force Basic Training. LIES! But that's a whole other story. Ultimately, I was happy for Toni and wanted her happiness more than anything. I also didn't want her to make the same mistake I made by rushing into something as serious as a marriage before really getting to know the guy.

Toni had been playing the dating game for years, but in the past, she could never find someone who wanted more than just booty calls, and I never understood why. Toni was gorgeous, smart, funny, and secure. As far as I was concerned, men should've been lining up to wife her, but for some reason, she only ended up dating losers. It seemed like things were finally looking up for her in the romance department though, so I was super excited for the possibilities in store for her.

"Girl, I am so happy you found someone who makes you happy. If anyone deserves to find love, it's you, and I can't wait to meet my future brother-in-law," I said.

"Great! Because I'm planning the engagement party soon and you definitely need to be there."

"Girl, you know I wouldn't miss it. But, listen. I have to get ready to go downstairs to this conference. Talking to you, I done messed around and lost track of time. The first session starts in fifteen minutes. I'll call you when I get back home, okay?"

"Okay. I'll talk to you soon. Enjoy, and make sure you get you a lil sumn sumn while you're in New York, okay?'

"Uhmmm, NO ... but I'll talk to you soon. Bye, Toni."

"Bye, Kia." Toni laughed, before disconnecting the line.

As I sat on the edge of the bed, David, my super fine neighbor and almost-fling while I was married to Kyle, crossed my mind. I shook my head as I thought about how I downplayed our recent interactions when I was talking to Toni. The truth is, David had been showing a lot of interest in picking up where things left off before Kyle got out of prison, but I was leery. While David was definitely eye candy and the chemistry was still there, I was focused on my career and having fun—not getting into new relationships. Picking things up with David would have certainly meant something serious, and I wasn't sure I was ready for any new commitments. So, I kept it cordial as much as I could when David and I crossed paths, no matter how much I secretly wanted to jump his bones.

My urge to get a taste of David was so strong that when Toni proposed the idea of a girls' trip to Paris, I was eager to get away and get David out of my head. So, shortly after moving into my new home, Toni and I treated ourselves to a 10-day vacation touring the UK, Italy, and France. It was a much-needed break from the States and we had the time of our lives. Anything you can think of doing in Europe—we did it. I'm talking shopping sprees in upscale boutiques, delicious cuisine in Five Star restaurants, site-seeing in beautiful cities, learning about the local culture, and the late nights clubbing and grinding on fine, European men. We had too much fun, and I was ready to book an encore. But Toni was engaged to be married. How would that change the dynamic of our friendship? Would that be our last girls' trip? I also couldn't help but wonder if Toni was moving too fast, just like I had.

When Kyle, proposed to me, it was nothing special, but I will never forget how special that moment made me feel. For the first time in my life, a man demonstrated his interest in me for the long term by asking me to be his wife. The best part? He wasn't doing it because I had hinted at it or because he felt obligated for religious purposes. Kyle proposed because he genuinely wanted me as his partner in life—at least that's how he made me feel.

Ever since I was a little girl, I'd always imagined a fairytale life for me where I'd be swept off of my feet by the perfect guy.

But it took a shotgun marriage to the "perfect" guy for me to realize there are no perfect guys, and women like me who live in fantasy worlds tend to get dealt reality in strong doses. My relationship with Kyle was built on lies and deceit. In fact, marrying Kyle was no doubt the biggest mistake of my life, and the more I thought about it, the more I began to worry that Toni was setting herself up to suffer the same fate.

But then I had to check myself. It was unfair to project my relationship woes on Toni's relationship. She could have found herself a perfectly upstanding man who genuinely loved her. And just because my ex was a loser, it didn't mean every man was. The truth was, I was pushing my fears of trusting a man again onto Toni's man, a man I'd never even met!

I shook my head. I had to stop before I messed around and jinxed Toni's relationship as I wallowed in the depths of my own relationship shortcomings. I needed to put my issues to the side and give Toni's fiancé a chance. If she loved him, I would love him too, and as long as he treated her well, we'd have no beef. My best friend was about to get married, and her happiness was all that really mattered.

I had made it through the last session of the day and was starving. One glance out the revolving doors in the hotel lobby let me know I wasn't heading outdoors for dinner. It was pouring outside, so I made my way to the hotel restaurant and sat at the bar for a drink and ordered some food to bring up to my room. Just as I finished ordering my drink, the refreshing scent of men's cologne began to waft through my nostrils. I turned my head and caught a glimpse of an extremely attractive man. He stood about 6'2" with a strong, athletic build. He was wearing a business suit, but I could see his solid frame penetrating through his clothing. His eyes were intensely dark; his low hair cut was edged up to perfection. His skin was a golden bronze tone, and his chiseled face was accentuated by high cheek bones, full lips, and a neatly trimmed beard and moustache. He appeared to be Middle Eastern.

He was very well dressed. His tailored suit was perfectly paired with a dusk-toned dress shirt and matching, dark grey designer shoes. A stunning diamond-encrusted Rolex adorned his wrist, but what really caught my eye was the perfect white teeth behind his gorgeous smile that made my heart skip a beat. It had been a little while since I'd been in the presence of a man with such exceptional taste and style. Add that to the maturity and sense of confidence he exuded, and he kind of reminded me of a model I'd once dated.

As he smiled at me, I quickly turned my head, hoping he didn't think I was staring at him. It was then that I had a flashback of my first escapade with my ex-husband. I'd met Kyle during a road trip to the beach, but our relationship took off in a hotel. The thought made me wonder, what was it with me and men in hotels?

The handsome man rose from his seat at the bar and headed to the stool right next to me. I tried to play it cool, hoping he wouldn't try to speak to me but also hoping he would.

"Excuse me, but I just arrived here and I'm starving. You wouldn't have any recommendations for food here, would you?"

Oh my god, he's talking to me. I considered ignoring him but decided against it. I didn't want to be rude.

"No, I'm sorry but I've never been here before. I ordered the steak and baked potato if that helps. Can't really go wrong with that," I said, then smiled. As I took in the gorgeous stranger again, I almost did a double take. He wasn't just fine; he was fine-fine! *Damn, Nakia. Calm down. Let's not act like you've never seen a good-looking man before.*

"Thanks, Nakia." Then, he turned to the bartender. "I think I'll do the steak and baked potato as well."

Wait, how does he know my name?

"How do you know my name?" I asked bluntly.

"I don't know. Magic?" he smiled, showing a slight dimple on his left cheek.

"Not, funny. Seriously, how do you know my name?"

He stood up and positioned himself so that he was standing right in front of me. My heart rate began to increase. I wasn't scared though. I was intrigued. Then, he smiled, and pointed to the label on my chest, grazing it slightly with his fingertips. I tried not to shudder from the tingle his light touch sent through me.

"It says, 'Hi, my name is Nakia' on your name tag."

"Oh," I replied with a slight smile. I felt dumb. I'd totally forgotten about the nametag I'd put on during the networking segment of the conference.

"I'm Amir," he said, smiling as he extended his hand to shake mine.

"Nice to meet you, Amir. My name is Nakia, but I guess you know that."

"It's a pleasure to meet you, Nakia. A beautiful name for an equally beautiful woman. Do you mind if I dine with you this evening? I'd much rather be in your company than spend my time alone."

"Well, I had already ordered my food to go, but I guess I can tell the waiter I'll have it here." Against my better judgment, I agreed to have dinner with Amir. It had been a little while since I'd been in the company of an attractive man and Amir had piqued my curiosity.

He appeared to be a bit older than me, possibly in his mid-30s, and everything about him was mesmerizing.

"Great. In exchange for your company, I'll take care of your meal."

"Nah, I'm good. I can handle my bill. But thanks for the offer."

"Well, I'm sure you can handle your meal. I just wanted to thank you for obliging my dinner request, but, as you wish."

"So, are you here for the conference?" I asked, trying to change the subject. I also wanted to switch to a more professional tone before I got too lost in his looks.

"Yes, I am actually. I arrived a little late, however, so, I missed today's events. Did I miss anything important?"

"No, not really," I grinned. "If you've been to one, you've been to them all."

The truth was, I only attended conferences because it was a way to travel on someone else's dime. It was also a way to get out of the mundane routine that was work, eat, sleep, repeat. While the law firm was a great place to work for the pay and benefits, everything else was pretty lame. So, whenever the opportunity to attend a conference came along, I jumped at it.

"So, Miss Nakia, are you an attorney?"

"I am. I work as a contract lawyer for a firm in D.C. We mainly work on government contracts."

"Oh, okay. So, you have access to all those top-secret documents and what not, huh?"

"No, not really," I laughed. "The documents I work with are typically very boring. Are you an attorney as well?"

"Yes, I'm an estate attorney. I'm a founding partner of a firm based out of Virginia. So, not too far from D.C."

"Oh, okay. Small world. I'm actually from Richmond. Well, Jersey originally, but I spent all of my teenage years in Richmond. My parents still live there."

"Yeah, definitely a small world. I'm originally from the West Coast—L.A., to be exact, but I moved to the East Coast shortly after law school. After working for some time in Philadelphia, a colleague and I started our own firm in Williamsburg. My work is not exactly exciting either, though. Since I deal with estates, the majority of my work is with rich, old people on the verge of death, so while I'm doing well business-wise, Williamsburg is not the most exciting place to live. Now that I think of it, I kind of wish I would've settled in Richmond. Maybe I would've run into you sooner." Amir smiled at me flirtatiously.

How, cute. He's flirting with me. "Sir, I doubt we run in the same circles, especially since I'm guessing you're older than me. I don't think you would've run into little old me."

"Are you calling me old, Nakia?" he teased before flashing his pearly whites.

"No, I can just tell you're more mature than I am, and we probably would never have just run into each other, same city or not."

"Uh, huh…" he replied, gazing intently into my eyes.

I turned my head to avoid his gaze. Amir was giving me butterflies, and the feeling was starting to make me nervous.

The bartender arrived with our food. I welcomed the distraction, as I dressed my baked potato and seasoned my food with some salt and pepper. We ate for a while in silence, but even though I wasn't looking at him, I could tell he was looking at me.

"Can you stop?" I asked.

"Stop, what?" Amir asked innocently.

"Stop looking at me. You're making me nervous."

"I can't help it."

My face began to flush with heat. This man was making me feel things I hadn't felt in a minute.

"You know you're gorgeous. How could I not stare at you?"

"Well, it's rude," I replied, pretending as if I was annoyed. The truth was, I was becoming more and more curious about Amir by the minute, and if I didn't calm myself down, I had a feeling something was going down in one of our hotel rooms that night. Then, I checked myself. Why couldn't I invite a man to my room for a nightcap? It was nothing to be ashamed of. I was grown, single, and I had needs that I was confident Amir was more than equipped to fulfill. So, at that moment I decided to lighten up and enjoy dinner. If it led to something else, then it did. I deserved a little action. As I considered the possibilities of a night with Amir, I couldn't help but smile. If I ended up in bed with Amir, I'd be doing everything I told Toni I wasn't there to do.

"Can I ask you a question?" Amir asked, interrupting my thoughts.

"Well, technically, asking me can you ask me a question is a question." I smiled, looking into his eyes.

"Yeah, you're right. But, look. I'm not trying to be forward. But I am interested in you, and though I can see you visibly trying to hide it, I know you are interested in me too."

"Oh, really? What makes you think I'm feeling you?" I replied seductively.

"I'm a grown man, Nakia. I know when the feeling is mutual," he replied, matching the intensity in my gaze.

The rest of dinner was a blur, but it seemed like it was only moments later that Amir and I were in my hotel room, ripping each other's clothes off. Amir was fully unclothed, and I was down to my panties and bra when Amir turned me around and pinned me against the wall. His erection was pressing against the lace on the back of my panties. It felt hard and thick, just the way I liked it. I could feel my moistness pooling in the center of my panties as my nipples began to harden, protruding through the cups of my bra. As if on cue, Amir unhooked and removed my bra, then cupped both of my breasts from the back, his thumbs making a circling motion around my areolas. I moaned in pleasure. I was high on the energy exchange between us, and the excitement of the moment was orgasmic in and of itself.

"Pardon my French but damn, Nakia. Your body is all that girl. I knew it was fine in that dress you had on, but seeing you like this—let's just say you've definitely exceeded my expectations."

I could feel him getting even harder, if that was even possible, and I began to fantasize about how he would feel inside of me. Without another word, he maneuvered my panties until they were down around my ankles and entered my wetness from behind.

I moaned passionately.

His strokes were slow and deliberate at first before increasing in pace and intensity until he was rapidly drilling in and out of me while I held my palms to the wall for support. Just as I felt I was about to explode, he turned me around, got down on his knees, propped one of my legs over his shoulder, then buried his face in between my thighs, sucking passionately on the juices that streamed from me in abundance. I was in bliss. I hadn't been blessed like that in a while, and I was loving every moment of it. Electricity traveled through every part of my body, and I felt dizzy as my body began to climax. My moans seemed to turn him on even more, because he began to aggressively lick and suck on my clit, bringing me to a level of bliss I never knew was possible.

After I came down from my high and my body was calm, Amir led me to the bed. He laid down, and I placed myself in the reverse cowgirl position and eased myself onto his throbbing member slowly. He gripped my waist as I rode him, my cheeks slapping loudly against his body. I'd let go of every inhibition and was thoroughly enjoying myself as I moved my hips back and forth on top of him. His legs began to tense up and he moaned deeply as his own explosion began to overcome him. I slowed down my pace and began to move my hips in a circular motion before leaning forward and bouncing my ass slowly. I continued my rhythmic motion until I could feel myself exploding along with him.

I arched my back as both of our bodies came in unison, and when we were done, I turned around so I was facing him. After kissing his sensual lips passionately, I collapsed onto his chest in exhaustion, where we spent the next hour frozen in position until it was time for round two, three, and four. Our escapades didn't stop until almost five the next morning when both of us were too spent to move.

"Damn, that was good," I said, as I nestled close to him, my head resting on his chest.

"Yeah, definitely. You might be right about my age, love. You've worn this old man out."

"Cut it out, you are NOT old. To be clear, I never said you were old." We laughed.

"So, tell me more about yourself," I said.

"What do you want to know?"

"Well, for starters, why are you single?"

"I could ask you the same thing, but I guess I just haven't met someone who's captured my interest long enough for a commitment. Plus, I enjoy being a bachelor."

"Same."

"You enjoy being a bachelor?" he kidded.

"You know what I meant," I said before playfully hitting him across one of his biceps.

"So, do you have any sisters or brothers?"

"No. I'm an only child. It's just me and my parents."

"Any kids?" he asked.

I paused before answering as I thought about my miscarriage. It was a still a sore spot in my memory. "No—not anymore."

"I'm sorry," he replied sadly, seeming to understand what I meant.

"It was a miscarriage," I said. "I was stressed. My husband was incarcerated."

"Husband?" Amir asked curiously.

"I'm just getting over a divorce. We married young, and it didn't work out. The divorce, the miscarriage—it was the worst period of my life. I'm only just beginning to move on."

"I'm so sorry, Nakia. You didn't deserve any of that."

"Yeah, I know," I replied sadly.

As we lay in bed talking, I learned a lot about Amir's upbringing. He was raised by a single mom who was Black, but he stayed with his dad, who was Syrian, on the weekends until he passed away from cancer when Amir was 10. Amir was single, had no children, owned a home, was very committed to his career, and loved to travel; though he enjoyed being a bachelor, he was open to a relationship with the right woman.

As I lay in Amir's arms, a feeling of security I had not really felt since Jerell began to flood throughout my being. I couldn't help but wonder again for the millionth time how things would've been if I'd stuck things out with Jerell. My mother had run into Jerell at the mall sometime prior, and she'd given him my new number and address, but I hadn't heard from him. I wasn't really surprised though. I was sure someone as fine and good of a man as Jerell couldn't possibly be single. Still, I couldn't help but think about how crazy it was that as I lay there in a stranger's arms, all I could think about was my first love. Funny how the heart works.

"You know we can't lie here all morning, as much as I would love to," Amir said, interrupting my thoughts.

"Yeah, I know," I groaned, as I rolled over onto my back. It was already 7 in the morning, and the first session for the day's conference was scheduled to begin at 9. I pulled the sheet over my nude body as I sat up in bed and watched Amir stand to get dressed. His body was the definition of perfection. He was in perfect shape with a chiseled chest, washboard abs, and defined leg muscles. Oh, and that semi-erect thing hanging in between his legs was impressive as well. I could feel myself getting aroused as I stared at him. He caught my gaze and smiled.

"Okay, Nakia. If you insist," he said playfully, before diving back onto the bed and climbing on top of me underneath the sheet. I wrapped my legs around him, pulling him inside of me, and closed my eyes as I basked in the sensation. I loved the way he felt inside of me—something about it was so naughty, yet so right. I tightened my grip around him with my legs, forcing him deeper inside. He moaned as he began to pump in and out, while kissing my neck and breast passionately. My fingernails dug into his back, and I tried to hold back the pulsing, tingling sensation of bliss that was quickly overcoming me. "Amir," I moaned as my wetness began to spill over. Our attraction to each other and the way our bodies moved with each other was magnetic.

The chemistry between us just felt right. Amir was easy to talk to. He made me feel like I was in a safe space and could trust him. We had just met, but it was as if we had known each other for years. When we were done, Amir collapsed onto the bed beside me and quickly fell asleep, leaving me to my thoughts again. It was way past 9, but I didn't care. I was perfectly content with spending the rest of my time in New York in my hotel room with Amir, and that's exactly what we did. There was a hint of mischief in the air, as if I were a school girl playing hooky from school as we skipped the rest of the conference in exchange for hours of exploring each other's bodies uninterrupted, ordering room service, and then showering together in my hotel room. And while I didn't know what would come out of my rendezvous with Amir, I knew that even if we never saw each other again, he'd made my time in New York one of the most memorable moments I'd had in a long time.

It was 4 in the morning on the day both Amir and I were scheduled to check out and head home. We'd spent the rest of the conference in my hotel room. As I gazed at Amir while he slept, I couldn't help but wonder if there could be a future with us. It was strange because less than a week prior, I had no intentions of being in a relationship with anyone. But, it's something about good "D" that makes me vulnerable—it's like my kryptonite, because at that moment, Amir had me completely sprung. I was all the way open, and I couldn't fathom that weekend being the only time I'd get to have him in that way.

I began to imagine us in a relationship. Regardless of what I told myself about not jumping into another relationship so soon after my divorce, deep inside I knew I'd always long for the security and companionship that I got from a committed relationship. It was something about the feeling of having a man to call my own that excited me, and no matter how I tried to commit to the single life, being in a relationship was never really too far from my thoughts.

"What you thinking about, love?" Amir asked. I hadn't realized he'd awakened.

"Oh, nothing much. Just wondering if I'll ever see you again."

"Well, that depends on you. Do you want to see me again?"

I sighed. The question was difficult. Yes, I'd definitely be open to spending more time with Amir, but I was also terrified about the potential of being hurt again the way I'd been by Kyle. Also, the fact that things were starting with Amir in pretty much the same way things did with Kyle made me nervous. I didn't want to make the same mistake twice.

"I would definitely be open to spending time with you again. But I can't help but wonder if we should just leave this at this, you know? Whatever happens, this weekend will always be special to me. I don't want to ruin this with unnecessary complications."

When Amir didn't respond, I looked over at him to see if I could read his expression. His eyes were closed, but I could tell he was awake and probably thinking. I decided to let things be as they were. We could talk more later. Then, I turned over and closed my eyes to get some sleep before checkout time. A few hours later, I awoke to find myself alone in my hotel room. Amir was nowhere in sight.

At first, I considered he may have just gone to get us some breakfast, but as time passed and it got closer to check out, I realized that I'd been played. Amir wasn't coming back. We'd had fun, but playtime was over, and it was time for us to move on with our lives. Even though I had convinced myself that I wasn't in the market for anything more than a fling, something in me felt sad that I'd never see him again. While I knew the majority of our time spent together was sexual, I still felt like Amir and I had bonded on a level more than sex. Either way, I chalked it up to being no more than a *few days stand*, and it was clear Amir had done the same. I hurried to get dressed and pack my things, then took one final glimpse at the room I'd spent the last two days sexing in. Then, I walked out the door, leaving it all behind.

CHAPTER 2

I had just settled into my seat on the train when my cell phone rang. It was from a number I didn't recognize, and for a moment, I wondered if it was Amir. But then I remembered that we'd never exchanged numbers, and I quickly pushed the thought out of my head.

"Hello?"

"Nakia? Hey, it's David."

"Hey. How did you get my phone number?"

"You gave me your number that day I saw you after you first moved into your house, and I have to be honest, I've been wanting to call you ever since."

Wow, this is unexpected. It felt weird hearing his voice, especially after I'd literally spent the last 48 hours have amazing sex with a man I didn't know. It was also awkward, considering how close we'd gotten while Kyle was in prison.

"I thought maybe we could link up since we're neighbors. I just think it's crazy how after your divorce and all, you ended up moving right next to me. That *can't* be a coincidence. It's almost like fate brought us back together."

I hesitated before responding. During our sexless fling, we never spent time at his home. I didn't even know where it was, so it was rather ironic that I ended up moving into his neighborhood of all places. Maybe he was right. Maybe it was fate. "Sure. I'd love to get together. When do you want to meet?"

"Well, how about dinner at my place tonight? I'll cook."

"You cook? Wow, I didn't know that."

"Yeah, I thought I told you. To be honest, I'm actually a pretty good cook."

"Well, I look forward to finding out for myself. I'm actually on my way home from New York, but I should be home in time for dinner. What time should I come over?"

"Around 6 is good for me, how about you?"

"Okay. I'll see you at 6. I'll bring some wine."

"Great! Sounds like a date. I'll see you a little later, Angel Face."

I smiled as I remembered his nickname for me. "Okay, I'll see you later, Handsome Face."

After I ended my call with David, I immediately scolded myself. *What in the world is wrong with me? What am I supposed to accomplish by meeting with David?* Granted, we'd managed to keep things platonic while spending time with each other when Kyle was locked up, but as a single woman, would I really be able to just be David's friend? It didn't help that from the sound of it, David was definitely interested in being more than that. I thought about my conversation with Toni a few days prior. I hadn't been completely honest with her about my interactions with David. I wasn't sure I'd been completely honest with myself either.

Ever since David had found out that I'd moved in a few houses down from him, we'd "conveniently" ran into each other at the complex parking lot, the local grocery store, and the gas station on several occasions. I was starting to think that he was following me, and I kind of liked it. The first time I saw him at the complex, I was on my way to Ocean City for the weekend, so we didn't have much time to talk, but we did catch up a bit. He apologized for his fight with Kyle at the funeral, and then we exchanged phone numbers, and I told him I'd be in touch. I lied, however. Something about connecting with David scared me a little. It was literally weeks after my divorce from Kyle, and everything about David reminded me of my time with Kyle. I was trying to make Kyle a distant memory, so being with David was a challenge I wasn't willing to take on initially. But whenever we ran into each other, I couldn't deny the spark between us.

What really sealed the deal for me was the time I caught a glimpse of him working out in the gym at our complex. He was wearing a wifebeater and grey sweatpants, and let's just say his print was hard to ignore. In fact, he was so distracting that I decided against working out and turned around and headed back to my house before he could see me. Since that day, I fantasized about being with him and seeing where things could go between us, but fear always prevented me from calling him. So, in a way, I was relieved when David called me and invited me to dinner. The timing was a bit off base, considering my interactions with Amir, but maybe it was worth a shot.

I made it home around 5 PM with just enough time to hop in the shower and get ready for my dinner date with David. After my shower, I rummaged through my closet before settling on some dark denim jeans, a black blouse with a swoop collar in the front that accentuated my breasts, a Gucci belt, and some YSL heels that I had splurged on in Paris. I pulled my long, mid-back length hair up into a bun, threw on some hoop earrings and a dab of makeup, grabbed a bottle of wine from the kitchen, then headed out the door to walk over to David's house. It was six on the dot when I rang his doorbell.

"Hey, Angel Face," David greeted me with a smile after opening the door.

We embraced, and from the tightness of his grip, I could tell he missed me. The way he held me was so sensual and intentional that it caused a quick flash of heat to surge though my body. That moment brought me back to how I felt the first time I met him. But those feelings were too much too soon, and I appreciated the distraction coming from the kitchen. A delicious aroma tickled my nostrils. I can't say that I expected David to be a good cook, but my nose could tell he knew exactly what he was doing. -

"So, in my haste to get you over here, I totally forgot to ask you what you liked to eat. I took my time and whipped up some-thing special. So, I hope you like it. We are having traditional New Orleans-style gumbo paired with sweet honey cornbread, and Southern sweet tea with lemon. But first, for an appetizer, I have some sweet and spicy Creole tiger shrimp with a sweet chili and sriracha sauce. I hope you're not allergic to seafood. I'm pretty sure I've seen you eat seafood in the past."

"No, I'm not allergic to seafood, and wow, you really outdid yourself tonight," I replied as I watched him plate our shrimp appetizer.

"I told you I know what I'm doing in the kitchen, but I figured you'd doubt me, so I decided to show off a little bit."

"Hmm, I see. So, how do you know how to cook Creole food? I thought you were Dominican?"

"I am. My father was Dominican. My mother is Creole. Her family hails from Louisiana and Mississippi, so she taught me how to cook at an early age."

After David was seated, he said a quick grace, and we both began to eat our appetizers. I could tell David was watching me while I ate.

"So, how does it taste?" David asked after my first few bites of shrimp.

"Delicious! I thought I knew how to throw down in the kitchen, but you clearly have me beat. The shrimp are fantastic. I can't wait to taste the gumbo."

"Say no more," David replied as he headed to the kitchen to plate our gumbo and cornbread. After he set out plates on the table, he poured us both a glass of sweet tea and then sat down to join me.

"So, do you speak Spanish?" I asked between bites.

"No. Not at all. I only have the Dominican looks. To be honest, I don't know much about that side of my family. My father was a deadbeat, and he died a few years ago, so I literally know nothing about him or his family, nor do I have any relationships with any of them."

"Yes, I remember you telling me that awhile back. I always feel sad for people when I find out they didn't get to grow up with both of their parents. I can't imagine not having a relationship with my father."

As an only child who grew up with both her parents in a middle-class neighborhood, I know most people find me privileged. I did not think of myself in that way when I was younger but as I've gotten older, I've encountered so many people who had rough childhoods, almost always with single moms who struggled to make ends meet. I'm so thankful for what I had. My parents weren't super wealthy by any means, but they both had good paying jobs and college degrees, and we never went without. I guess you never really know how good you have it until you learn about the experiences of others.

As we both ate, I couldn't help but feel like I'd placed myself in a dilemma. On more than one occasion during dinner, David hinted at wanting to be more than friends. While part of me was saying "absolutely not," another part of me wanted to test the waters with him. I guess I really didn't know myself or what I wanted as much as I thought I did. I still had a lot of work I needed to do on myself and forming a relationship with David when it hadn't even been a year since my divorce from

Kyle seemed reckless. I needed to find a way to tell David that I enjoyed spending time with him, but I needed to take it slow. I wasn't ready for a commitment. There was still a lot of soul searching I needed to do for myself. As if reading my mind, David broke the silence.

"What are you thinking?" he asked before taking a bite.

"Honestly? I was thinking about us. I don't want you to get the wrong idea about tonight and my intentions."

His demeanor changed as he placed his fork on his plate. A puzzled expression formed on his face before he asked, "Why do you think I have the wrong idea? You *are* feeling me, aren't you?"

"Yes, David. You're an amazing man. I can never repay you for your friendship during the most challenging and chaotic time of my life. You were there for me when I needed you, and I will forever be grateful. But if I'm being real, I've changed a lot since then. I'm also trying to be a lot more careful with my heart. I don't want to rush into a new relationship when my divorce is still so fresh. I want to explore the world and myself and figure out who I am before I commit to something new. I just don't think I'm ready to be someone's girlfriend, and I know that's what you want."

He reached across the table and placed his hand over mine as he looked deeply into my eyes.

"Nakia, you make me happy. When I'm with you, nothing else matters. It's like I'm on cloud nine. You're funny, intelligent, independent, and incredibly sexy. But most of all, you're important enough to me for me to wait until you're ready. I just want your friendship. I want to spend time with you. You say you're a different person? Well, I'm willing and ready to get to know you all over again. I'm here and I'm patient, but most of all I just want you back in my life on the regular. If you keep it real with me, I promise to do the same. That's all I'm asking for."

He softly caressed my hand before slowly pulling his hand away. I was speechless. How could I deny David a friendship? He'd been there for me when I needed him, and it seemed he was asking me to do the same for him. While I was hesitant to embark on something new, even just a friendship, I couldn't deny the warmth and comfort I felt around him. David had always treated me well, so what did I have to fear? I had to learn how to stop projecting my experiences with Kyle on every man in my life. As I thought about what David said, the sound of Sade's "Lovers Rock" began to fill the room. After putting the stereo remote on the table, he rose and began walking toward me.

"Can I have this dance?" he asked, extending his hand to me.

I nodded.

As David pulled me close to him and I wrapped my arms around his neck, I felt a genuine sense of comfort. I lay my head on his chest and closed my eyes, basking in such a simple but intimate moment. It was almost as if David was too good to be true, and that concerned me. But I also considered the possibility that I'd gotten so accustomed to being treated like shit that I didn't know how to act when someone genuinely had my best interests in mind. While I didn't doubt that Kyle loved me in his own special way, I knew that he was never shown how to love properly, and that's why he made so many mistakes with me. I also knew that until I was able to truly forgive Kyle for hurting me, and most importantly, forgive myself for allowing Kyle to continue to hurt me, I would never be able to have a healthy relationship with any man. It was then that I considered finding a therapist. I had too much unaddressed trauma that I needed to confront, and ignoring it was holding me back.

After the song ended, David led me back to the dinner table.

"Would you like some dessert? I've prepared some strawberry cheesecake."

"Wow. Have I told you that you've outdone yourself this evening, Mister?" I laughed. "Yes, I'd love some cheesecake."

After we finished dessert, I began to notice how stiff my neck was. I decided it must have been from falling asleep wrong on the train, but the pain was beginning to increase and was beginning to destroy my good mood.

"Hey, you wouldn't happen to have any Tylenol, would you? I'm getting a little sore," I said, as I rubbed my neck and shoulders intensely.

"No, I don't actually. But I do have something better."

David rose from the table and headed towards a room in the back. He returned a few moments later with a bottle of oil of some sort.

"Let me show you one of my other skills," he said, before massaging some of the oil into the palms of his hands, before getting into position behind me. He started to deliver the best neck and shoulder massage I'd ever experienced. His hands melted into my body, causing instant relaxation. The knots in my neck and shoulders dispersed as if defeated by his grip. I was in total ecstasy while his hands moved across my skin expertly. He added just the right amount of pressure to decrease the pain that was emanating from beneath my skin. I closed my eyes and relaxed as the sounds of Floetry's "Say Yes" began to play through his speakers.

As David put in work on my neck and shoulders, I couldn't help but want more. It was like his touch was an aphrodisiac, and the more he touched and rubbed, the more I wanted him. Maybe it was the fact that I drank more wine than sweet tea during dinner, but whatever it was, it was becoming hard for me to deny him.

When the song finished, I stood to face David. I reached up to touch the side of his face before pulling it close to mine. I bit his bottom lip softly, before beginning to passionately kiss him, letting every emotion I had buried inside of me for him escape. As we kissed, I pushed him backward toward the sofa, and once he was seated, I straddled his lap facing him and resumed kissing him. His lips were smooth and plush, and he kissed with just the right amount of tongue and wetness to let me know that the moment was meant to be. I could feel his hardness through my jeans as I grinded on top of him, fully clothed, and I loved the way he allowed me to be in control.

I kissed his lips, before reaching down to unbuckle his jeans. My hands manipulated his hardness, and a sea of moans escaped his lips. He was turning me on. Moisture was building between my legs, and my body began to feel like it was on fire. I took off my shirt, and David did not hesitate to remove my bra. I stared into his eyes for a moment, searching for hints of what he was thinking. Without a word, he pulled me closer and took one of my breasts into his mouth. He nibbled and sucked voraciously, and I continued to stroke him, increasing in pace. My panties were soaked, and I was sure it was spilling through my jeans. He stood me up to remove my jeans and panties before taking off his shirt, jeans, and boxers. We both stood looking at each other in awe of our glory as if it were the moment we'd been waiting for all our lives. David was blessed. He may have been holding more than any man I had ever been with, and as I took in the beauty of his large, chiseled body, I couldn't wait to feel him inside of me.

As if reading my thoughts, David picked me up and carried me into his bedroom before lowering me gently onto his bed. Then he parted my legs before his tongue dived deep inside of me. As he sucked and slurped, it felt as if we had entered another world made just for us. I was on the verge of my climax. I gripped the back of his head to hold it place and to prolong the moment, but the passion that had been building up was too strong, and as I let myself go, I was sure my moans could be heard throughout the entire complex.

After I was finished, David climbed on top of me and entered me slowly. I parted my legs wider to allow all of him into me. He took his time, stroking in and out of me slowly and with intention, as if with each stroke he was basking in the essence of me. His rhythm was steady and passionate, each stroke seeming to be deeper and more intentional than the last. The way our bodies felt intertwined was like a love reawakened that was finally able to be free. David wasn't just sexing me, he was making love to every part of me, and I basked in it.

Tears of bliss escaped my eyes as we both came in unison, and when we were done, he held me in his arms. The only word I can use to describe how I felt was "stuck." I wasn't up nor down from my high, but instead, somewhere in the middle. But as David's breathing slowed, I could tell he was falling asleep. But I was wide awake. *What am I doing? That's two men back to back. Didn't I just tell him that I wasn't ready for any of this? Why would he put it on me like that? Why couldn't he have been mediocre? It would make what I have to do so much easier.*

Once I was sure David was completely out, I slowly slid out of the bed then tiptoed into the living room to get dressed. I grabbed my house keys and quietly exited the house. I knew I was wrong for leaving him like that, but my feelings were all over the place, and I needed to be in my own home to gather myself. So, as I closed the door behind me, I quietly whispered, "I'm sorry." Then, I walked home in the dark, unsure of everything.

CHAPTER 3

It was a Friday and my first day back at work since the conference. I wasn't anticipating all the work waiting for me, but I
knew it would be a busy day. Luckily, I'd have the weekend to
recuperate and sort out my crazy antics from the past few days.

"Hey, Janice. How are you?" I greeted our receptionist.

"Good morning, Nakia. How was the conference?"

I thought for a moment before I spoke, remembering that
I'd only actually attended one day of the conference. "Great!
There were some excellent speakers there," I lied. "Do I have
any messages?"

"No, no messages. But Brad in HR would like you to come
to his office. We have a new intern working in your department,

and I think he'd like you to show her the ropes. Her name is Jordyn."

Great. Now I'll have play tour guide today and deal with someone else when all I want is to do my work in peace and leave. I tried not to roll my eyes. "Okay, I'll head over once I drop off my things in my office. Thanks, Janice."

After dropping of my belongings in my office, I headed toward the human resources office. Upon entering, I caught a glimpse of a stunning young woman. From the look of all the men idly hanging around from other departments, I could tell she'd caught their eye as well. She was tall, at least 6 feet, with long black wavy hair that fell past her shoulders. Her skin was light brown, which was in stark contrast to her piercing dark brown eyes like a raven's. She was dressed in an all-black pant-suit, with a black blouse underneath her blazer. She wore zebra print open toe shoe boots, light makeup, and beautiful pearl ear-rings that changed color, depending on how the light hit them.

"Hello, you must be Jordyn. I'm Nakia," I said as I stood in front of her and extended my hand to shake hers.

"Hi, Nakia. Nice to meet you. Thank you for being so kind to show me around today. I appreciate it. I know you're probably busy," she replied in a noticeably English accent.

"No worries. I'm happy to help," I said. "Will you be in the vacant office next to mine?"

"I think so. The office next to the copy room?"

"Yes, that's the one. Follow me." I intentionally ignored Brad. He always rubbed me the wrong way. According to whispers by the water cooler, Brad had slept with almost every young female attorney who worked at the firm, past and present. It was also rumored that he often offered higher starting salaries for the more attractive attorneys. Either way, he wasn't there when I applied for my position, and I'm glad I never really had to cross paths with him. He seemed like a certified creep as far as I was concerned.

"So, I'm assuming from your accent that you're British?"

"Yes, I was born and raised in London, although my father is American."

"Oh?" I asked. "How did your parents meet?"

"My father was in the Air Force," Jordyn said. "They met when she was working at the American Embassy. They moved to D.C after he retired, and I moved here to attend law school."

"Oh, wow. It seems like you've led an exciting life. How are you liking it here so far?"

"I love the area so far and school is going pretty well. I am quite nervous about this internship though. I don't want to mess anything up. So please, go easy on me!"

"Trust me, I've been in your shoes before, and I know how it is. Your time here will be a valuable learning experience that you'll look back on and be thankful for. I know how important it is to make an impression in a male-dominated industry. But have no fear. I am here to help you out. From one Black woman to another, I know the importance of helping each other out." Jordyn seemed to have a great personality, and I was slowly starting to come around to the idea of having someone around the office I could help mold. "I'm sure you'll be an excellent attorney. On a side note, have you ever considered modeling? You definitely have the height and looks for it."

Jordyn laughed. "Thank you. I actually modeled throughout college, but it wasn't really for me. I'm kind of clumsy, and let's just say walking the runway isn't really one of my strong suits."

"Got it." I laughed. "Well, here's my office," I said, gesturing toward an empty seat at my desk. "Have a seat, and we can get started."

"Sure, let me just run next door to my office and grab my laptop. I'll be right back."

She seems nice. As the only Black attorney in the entire office and one of the few Black employees, it felt nice to see another brown face. Jordyn seemed cool, and I was looking forward to getting to know her. By the time I helped her with logging in and gave her a tour of the building, it was time for lunch. The day was going by fast, and I was kind of relieved by the distraction from my thoughts and regular work routine. However, the distraction from all the mess in my head was short lived, because I returned from lunch to a voice message from David.

Hey, Nakia ... Well, I guess I was kind of disappointed that you left without saying goodbye. Did I do something wrong? I don't know. Sorry for calling you at work like this. I tried your cell phone and didn't get a response. I just wanted to make sure you were okay. Call me when you get off ... I'll talk to you soon.

Guilt immediately took over me and I felt terrible; however, I didn't know how to deal with my feelings for David. I was terrified at the potential of involving myself with someone who could hurt me like Kyle. Sure, David has not shown any signs of ill will, but neither did Kyle in the beginning. I couldn't fathom another heartbreak, so I ignored him. In order to avoid any possible negative outcomes, I decided my best course of action would be to just forget that night with David happened and go along with my regular routine. I didn't have time for the complications that came with starting a new relationship. I needed to focus on myself and my career, and that's exactly what I did.

Luckily for me, Jordyn proved to be a valuable distraction. It was almost as if she were a project for me. I took her under my wing, and we basically began to spend most of our free time together both during and after work. We frequented several wine bars in the area and even went shopping at Tysons Corner on occasion. Jordyn had a carefree attitude and was easy to get along with. I admired her free spiritedness. I'd always wanted a kid sister, and Jordyn played the role wonderfully. Aside from showing her the ropes at work, I gave her advice on next steps in her career and was a listening ear for her to talk to about her problems. Directing my attention to her helped me to take my mind off my recent escapades, and it felt good to be in the company of another "girlfriend."

In the past, I only really had Toni, but we didn't get to spend time together as much since we lived in two different states. Since Jordyn arrived, things had fallen back into a regular routine. I was enjoying work and hanging out with Jordyn, and life was drama free—just how I liked it. At first, David still continued to call, even though I never answered. I felt bad each time I saw his name flash across my caller ID, but I also didn't feel obligated to speak to him. Eventually, the calls stopped, and I was able to put him out of my mind completely.

It was a Friday night, and I'd just arrived home from work. As I undressed and changed into some shorts and a t-shirt, my cell rang. It was Toni. I'd been meaning to call her, but irregular phone calls were the norm for our friendship. Due to our busy schedules, we could go several weeks or even a month without talking or seeing each other; but whenever we finally would link up, it was as if we never missed a beat. That's what made our friendship so special. We understood each other, and time apart did not affect our relationship. Other friends in my past would have never understood the long spells between communication. This was the major reason why my circle of friends was small.

Toni and I hadn't spoken since my time in New York, and I'd been wanting to connect with her about the wedding planning, especially since I was the maid of honor. "Hey, Toni. What's up?" I answered the phone.

"Hey, Kia. I'm doing okay. Sorry, I haven't called you. I've been dealing with a few things."

"You don't sound so good. What's going on?" I could tell from Toni's voice that something was bothering her.

"A little over a week ago I had a break-in—"

"Wait! What? A break-in? Toni, why are you just now telling me this?" I cut her off.

"I'm sorry. It took me a while to process it, but I'm fine. I wasn't home when it happened and nothing important was taken. It just shook me up a little bit. I'd spent the night at my cousin's house after her baby shower, and when I returned home the next morning, my door was ajar. AJ was away on a business trip, so I went to my parents' house until he returned. As soon as I called him, he caught the next flight to come be with me. Girl, it's just been hectic setting up alarm systems, changing locks. I guess I've been a bit stressed, but I'm sorry I didn't call you sooner."

"Don't worry about it, best friend. I'm just glad you're okay—that's what's most important."

"Yeah, me too. But enough about all the depressing stuff. What have you been up to? Any new love interests?"

"No, no new love interests. I'm doing well, and I'm happily single. Just been focusing on work, and being a mentor of sorts to the new girl?"

"New girl?"

"Oh, yeah. Jordyn. She's a new intern at the firm. She's a young, beautiful sista. I've been showing her the ropes and just being a friend to her. She's new to the area."

"Oh, that's nice. I'm glad you were able to find a female friend near you—Lord knows I shouldn't be your only female friend."

We laughed. "Yeah, especially since you're not nearby. But I've been wanting to talk to you anyway. I want to help you with the wedding planning. I'm sure you have a list of things for your maid of honor to do, and it just so happens I'll be in town tomorrow at my parents' for the weekend. They're throwing a cookout, and of course, you're invited. Maybe we can hang out and get some planning done."

"Aww, girl, I wish. But we'll have to get together another time. AJ and I are headed to Aruba tomorrow morning for a week. He surprised me with the tickets right after the break-in. He feels bad about not being here when the house was broken into and wanted to cheer me up. I have this huge project I'll be working on for about six weeks once we return from our trip, so I'm postponing wedding planning until I'm finished with the work stuff. That'll make it easier for me to focus."

"Aww, that's sweet. You do what you gotta do, girl. We'll link up when you're free. But back to Aruba—girl—I wish I had someone to whisk me on a tropical getaway!"

"Hmmm, didn't you just tell me that you were happily single?"

"Yeah, yeah, yeah," I said before we both burst out into laughter. While I was trying to be happily single, I did wish I had someone to surprise me with a tropical getaway or to just outright spoil me. In all of my time married to Kyle, we'd never been anywhere. No vacations, no big surprises—nothing. Somehow, listening to other people's relationship joys only made me further regret the time I'd wasted with him.

"Well, smooches, have a safe trip Toni and don't drink too much," I said, laughing.

"Love you bunches, and I will do just the opposite," she replied before hanging up.

After the call, loneliness hit me even more. I was a beautiful, successful Black woman, and I had no one to come home to. On top of that, I had a perfectly good, handsome man who was interested in me, but I was too afraid to test the waters with him. I couldn't help but think that love and happiness for me wouldn't come around for a long time, and that was enough to make me want to curl up and cry.

CHAPTER 4

It was a Saturday morning, and I had just arrived at my parents' home in Richmond for their annual summer cookout. The weather was perfect, a warm 80 degrees, and the sun was shining. It felt good to be back home. I entered the house through the back door and came upon my father in the kitchen.

"Hey, Daddy!" I said, walking with my arms outstretched to give him a hug.

"There's my girl," he replied with a big grin. "It's been awhile since you came to see your old pops."

"Yeah, I know. I'm sorry. I've just been busy at work. You know I get my hard-working attitude from you, Dad."

"Yeah, but don't work too hard. You have to make time for fun and family."

"Yes, I'll try to do better and come visit more. I miss y'all. Where's mom?"

"Oh, she drove to pick up a few things at the grocery store. You know your mom. I told her we have everything we need for the cookout, but she's always adding something to the menu at the last minute. Anyway, I'm about to head out into the yard and get the grill ready. Is your girlfriend Toni coming today? I feel like I haven't seen her since y'all graduated from college."

"Yeah, I guess it has been a while. But, no, Toni isn't able to come today. She's on vacation with her fiancé. Can you believe she's getting married?"

"Oh, wow. That's good news. Wow, all of y'all kids have really grown up. I remember the first time we met Toni during your freshman orientation at college. Time really flies," he said, shaking his head as he walked out to the backyard.

Time really did fly. It seemed like only yesterday was move-in day at college, and I was wondering how me and my new roommate, Toni, would get along. Now, years later, I'm newly divorced, and she's newly engaged. I also became saddened by the fact that my own marriage didn't last, and I wondered if I'd ever get my happily ever after. I hadn't seen or talked to Kyle since the day we signed the divorce papers, but I couldn't help but wonder how he was. Toni said she'd see him from time to time, and he always looked sad. She said he always had Kyle

Jr. in tow as well, so I secretly wondered if he'd gotten back with his son's mother. I could see how that would be easier than paying child support each month. I thought back to the day that she showed up at Kyle's door with news of him having a son, and I could tell by the way she looked at Kyle that she still had feelings for him. I didn't blame her though. I'd want to be with the father of my first child too.

No sooner had I thought about Kyle and Kyle Jr. that I began to think about my miscarriage and the child we could've had. Tears started to fall from my eyes. Why did I always torture myself? I headed to the bathroom to wash my face and exited just as my mother was coming into the house.

"Hey, baby. How long have you been here?"

"Hey, Mama," I said before giving her a kiss on the cheek. "Not long, maybe a half-hour. So, what do you need my help with?"

"You can start by getting those greens started. I figured I'd let you make your famous spicy greens."

"Okay, cool," I said with a smile. It felt good to be in the kitchen with my mother. It reminded me of when I was younger, and we'd cook Sunday dinner together. Our family was small, but Mama and I always went all out for dinner on Sundays even though it was just the three of us and the occasional guest or two.

"So, how is life in that townhome community you live in? Have you met anyone new?"

I really wasn't interested in telling my mother about any of my relationship drama. She would be so disappointed in my behavior, so even though my mother and I were close, I chose to keep my love life to myself.

"No, I haven't met anyone. To be honest, I've just been focusing on work. There's a new girl at my job who's interning, and I've kind of taken her under my wing. I really haven't had much time for anything else."

"Oh, that's nice. You should've invited her. Is she from the area?"

"Well, her name is Jordyn, She's actually originally from London, but her family lives in D.C.. Now that I think of it, I should've invited her. I guess it slipped my mind."

"Oh, okay. Well maybe next time. It's rare that I hear you mention any new friends. I was starting to think Toni would be stuck as your only friend for the rest of your lives." She laughed. "How is Toni doing anyway? I haven't seen her in a while."

I laughed. "Dad said the same thing. But Toni is doing very well, actually. I guess I forgot to tell you, but she's getting married. She and her fiancé left this morning to vacation in Aruba, which is why she wasn't able to come today."

"Oh, wow. Little Toni is getting married. That's good to hear. I wish her the best and look forward to my invitation to the wedding."

The rest of the morning flew by, and my mother and I cooked and prepared the house for our guests. Once the guests began to arrive, I ran upstairs to my bedroom to freshen up and changed my clothes. I had just returned downstairs to join everyone when I heard a familiar voice behind me.

"Hey, Nakia."

The familiar voice caused waves of excitement in the pit of my stomach. I turned around to see the first man I ever really loved, Jerell. I wanted to run up and embrace him, but I played it cool.

"Jerell? Wow, I didn't know you were coming today."

Jerell grinned. "Yeah, I saw your mom at the grocery store earlier today, and she invited me. She said it would be a nice surprise for you. I actually saw her about a month ago as well, and she told me you moved to Bowie, Maryland. She gave me your information, but I must have misplaced it. Anyway, it's nice to see you, Nakia."

"Yeah, likewise," I said before giving him a warm hug. As we released our embrace, I could feel butterflies in my stomach. He smelled so good, and the years had treated him well. He hadn't aged at all, and he looked finer than ever.

"Well, you're welcome to help yourself to a plate. I'm not hungry yet, so I'll be sitting at the table under the shade if you want to join me."

"Okay, I'll be over to catch up in a few."

Before I sat down, I made sure to head over to give my mother a quick word.

"Mama, why didn't you tell me you invited Jerell over?"

"Huh? Did I? Oh, yeah. I forgot all about it. I saw him at the grocery store earlier looking a little frail. I figured he could use a good meal. I'm sorry, baby. It totally slipped my mind," she replied with a slight grin.

"Yeah, I bet," I said, laughing. Then, I sat down to wait for Jerell.

A few moments later, he joined me at the table. As I watched him set his plate down, I kind of regretted not getting a plate for myself.

"Wow, I missed your mama's cooking, and are these your famous spicy collard greens I'm tasting?" Jerell asked after taking a couple of bites.

"Yeah, they are," I replied with a smile.

"Yeah, I definitely missed these too," he said, as he stuffed his face.

As I watched Jerell shovel food into his mouth like he hadn't had a home cooked meal in forever, I began to miss the times we shared. I used to cook for him every weekend. I couldn't help but miss our weekend routine of being cooped up in my old apartment, eating, and making love, and just being with each other. I still found it hard to get over the fact I'd let a good thing go so easily, especially on account of a man that turned out to be a waste of time.

"So, how have you been, Jerell? Are you still modeling?"

"Yeah, I'm still modeling. I'm also doing a little acting here and there. Nothing major, but professionally, I'm doing pretty good. How about you? I see you're finally an attorney. I'm glad to see all of your hard work has paid off."

"Yes, career-wise, things are good for me as well. That's basically all I've been focusing on since the divorce."

Jerell's expression seemed to sadden when I mentioned my divorce.

"I'm sorry things didn't work out for you in your marriage. I can't imagine how any man could let a good woman like you go so easily—but then again, I'll always regret not fighting for us like I should have. I often wonder if we'd be married with children by now."

"I think about that too. To be honest, I think the biggest mistake of my life was pushing you away. I don't know what was wrong with me other than being young, dumb, and naive. Now

I'm an almost-30 divorcée. In my rush to be married, I risked it all and lost."

I tried to keep the tears from forming in my eyes. I missed Jerell and everything we had, and I wanted him back in my life in some capacity. They say you never know what you've got until it's gone, and no truer words have been said. Of all the men in my life in the past few years, Jerell was the one that I would actually take the risk of starting a new relationship with. Being in his presence made me realize that deep down, I wanted that old thing back. At that moment I made the hasty decision to do what I had to do to get him back.

"Look, don't be down on yourself. We all make mistakes, but I believe everything happens for a reason. Every part of life is an experience that shapes who we'll become, so though I beat myself up about some of the choices I've made, I try not to live my life filled with regrets."

"Yeah, I guess that's a good way to think about it. But sometimes I wonder why I'm so reckless with my heart. I've made some decisions that have really made me ask myself, what the hell was I thinking?"

"Well, you've always been one to know what you want. Even though I'm older than you, I've always been able to learn from you. I think you were just sure of what you wanted from your future, and I hadn't yet caught up. While I was very much in love with you and knew one day I wanted you to be my wife, I don't think I was mentally prepared to be a husband at that time. But things change, and people mature. I guess it's all about timing."

"Yeah, it's definitely all about timing. That was the lesson I needed to learn, and I think I finally understand it now," I said, smiling.

Is all this talk about timing and learning lessons a hint that he wants that old thing back, too? I couldn't help but wonder if Jerell was showing signs that he was interested in pursuing a relationship with me again. Would my dreams finally come true? Was everything that I went through with Kyle just a lesson so I could realize I had everything I needed with Jerell?

"What are you over there smiling about?" Jerell asked.

"Oh, nothing." I hadn't realized I was smiling and probably looked stupid since I wasn't saying anything. "So, when's your next gig?" I asked, changing the subject.

"Well, I'm heading to LA next week to shoot a commercial and meet up with a few colleagues from overseas to see if I can get my face in front of the right people. I've also been working as a salesman at a car dealership near my place just to make sure I have a steady stream of income. They're really flexible with my hours and accommodate me when I have gigs, so it works out."

"Oh, okay. Well, you're definitely handsome enough. I know you have no problems selling cars and making your sales quota."

"Why does everyone think that?" he asked, laughing. "I promise you my looks have nothing to do with me being top salesman for the past three quarters. I work just as hard as everyone else," he replied while rolling his eyes teasingly.

"Yeah, yeah. I bet."

The rest of the day was spent catching up and playing card games with family. Jerell and I hung out the entire time and being around him again felt just like old times. Being around him brought back old memories. We reconnected as if no time had passed and my feelings for him were reigniting. After the cookout was over, he was kind enough to help me and my parents clean up. When it was time for him to go, I walked him to his car.

"So, what are you doing tomorrow? I'm here until Monday."

"Actually, I really don't have any plans. I was probably just gonna hang out, maybe hit up Sterling's and get a few drinks and food. That's what I typically do on Sundays when I don't have any other plans."

"Wow! I haven't been to Sterling's since we were together. How's the old crew doing over there?"

"Everyone's fine. The same people are there every weekend just like they were when we were there. Do you want to link up tomorrow evening and get some food and drinks? I'll probably head over there around 5."

"Sure! That sounds great. I'll go to church with my parents in the morning and then have lunch with them, but once we're done, I'll swing by Sterling's and we can hang out. I could use a few adult beverages."

"Alright, cool. I'll see you tomorrow then. Tell your mom thank you again for the invite. It was nice seeing everyone again."

"Okay, I will," I said before giving him a hug goodbye. It wasn't quite as long as I would've liked, but Jerell genuinely seemed happy to be around me again, and the fact that he wanted to link up the next day was promising. While I was excited about spending more time together, I couldn't help but feel excited about the possibility of rekindling things with him. I was quite familiar with his sexual appetite, and I knew once Jerell had a piece, he'd be all mine. For the moment, I was determined to make that happen.

I got home from church the next day around 1. After eating a light lunch of leftovers with my parents, I headed upstairs to my room to take a quick nap before I had to get ready to meet Jerrell at the sports bar. After my nap, I showered then threw on a crop top and some cut off shorts, added a little bit of makeup, and styled my hair down the way Jerell liked it. I sprayed a little bit of perfume and headed out the door to the bar.

I arrived at Sterling's before Jerell, and after saying hi to all the regulars I knew, I grabbed our favorite corner booth and waited for him. He arrived about ten minutes after I did and greeted me with a hug and a kiss on the cheek.

"Did you order anything yet?" he asked.

"No. I just got here a little while ago. I figured I'd wait for you."

A few moments later, the waiter came over. After ordering drinks and wings, Jerell joined me on my side of the booth, and we sat back and watched the game, chatting it up with some of the regulars we knew. Then, after we ate, we played a few rounds of pool before heading back to our booth for more drinks. By that time, I'd had about six drinks and I was feeling extremely loose and tipsy.

"Uh oh, I see that look in your eyes."

"What look?" I asked innocently.

"You know what look. You're wasted," Jerell said, laughing.

"I am not," I whined. The truth was, I was definitely feeling tipsy, and when I got tipsy, I became extremely flirtatious. While I definitely felt relaxed and knew I was safe with Jerell, I didn't want to begin acting like a fool. So, when the waitress came back over to ask if we wanted refills, I ordered a soda in an attempt to try to sober up a bit.

"You know, it almost feels like old times, being around you, Nakia. I've really missed this, especially when I was overseas. I thought about you constantly. Even once I knew it was over between us, I really couldn't bring myself to date anyone else or even be around other women for a long time because deep down, I always thought I'd get a call from you saying that you wanted us to start over. But the call never came, and I must admit, I was depressed for a long time."

I felt terrible hearing Jerell tell me how I broke his heart. As I reflected back to that time, I realized how badly I treated him. Not once while I was messing around with Kyle did I think about Jerell's feelings. I treated him like trash, and I knew if I wanted Jerell back in my life, I'd have to do a lot to make it up to him. But I had a plan.

After another hour of talking and hanging out at the sports bar, Jerell and I were finished, and I was ready to put my plan into action. While I wasn't completely sober yet, I was sober enough to know that I needed to act quickly to get Jerell in my grips if I wanted to make sure I spent the night at his place.

As we walked toward my car, I grabbed his hand. Just the feel of his strong hand over mine sent tingles through my spine. I missed his touch so much, and I couldn't wait to be in his arms the way I used to. Once we reached my car, I turned to face him.

"Sooooo ... what are you doing for the rest of the night?" I asked.

"Nothing, much. I'll probably just hit the sack. I have to be at work at 10 in the morning."

"Hmmm. I was asking because I wanted to know if you wanted some company. I promise I won't keep you up too late," I said flirtatiously, walking closer to him.

Jerell's expression changed. He looked sad and confused at the same time. For a few moments, he just looked at me and didn't say anything, like he was trying to find the right words to say. Finally, I spoke, to break the silence.

"What's wrong?"

He sighed. "Nakia, this is hard for me. For the longest time, I hoped the day would come when I'd have the chance to make you mine again and being with you yesterday and today definitely brought back a lot of good memories we shared. It felt so good to be around you and see you laugh—it felt just like old times. But I have to be honest. I'm in love with someone else. A few months ago, I reconnected with a girl I knew from overseas. She's here in the States now, and we've been seeing each other ever since. Things are getting serious, and I honestly see her as the woman I want to make my wife." He hesitated before continuing. "I'm sorry. I didn't mean to lead you on. I really just thought we were hanging out as friends."

Embarrassment paralyzed me. My face became overheated and flushed. The embarrassment quickly turned to anger before instantaneously turning to sadness. Self-sabotage swiftly crept in. *How could I be so dumb? Why would I assume that Jerell was single?* Not once did I consider that he might have been in a relationship, and even if he had told me beforehand, I wasn't sure it would've mattered. Once again, I was being selfish and putting my needs before his. At that point, I knew I didn't deserve Jerell at all.

I turned away from him to face my car so he wouldn't see the tears that were beginning to well in my eyes. I could feel him put his hand on my shoulder in an attempt to comfort me.

"Nakia, I'm so sorry. I didn't expect any of this. I guess I should've told you I was in a relationship up front. Maybe a part of me wanted to see where things would go with us, and for that, I'm truly sorry."

"It's okay. I understand," I said between sobs. I was no longer trying to hide the fact that I was crying. I was devastated, and I knew he knew it.

"Listen, do you need me to drive you home? I don't want you to drive back to your parents like this, especially since you've had a few drinks."

"I'm good. I'll be alright."

There was a short silence before Jerell spoke.

"Okay, well at least call me to let me know you got home okay. Again, I'm sorry, Nakia. I really wish things were different, but it seems like our time came and went. I'll always love you, and I want us to remain friends. I want us to be able to hang out—I mean, I hope we'd get to the point one day where I'd be able to introduce you to my lady and we can all hang out. You, me, and our significant others."

"Yeah, that would be nice," I said softly. But I was lying. There was no way I could hang out with Jerell anymore, knowing how I felt about him, and I definitely couldn't be around him and his girl. Nope. This would be the last time I'd spend with Jerell. It had to be, for my own personal sanity.

I watched as Jerell pulled out of the parking lot and drove down the road and out of sight. I began to sob even harder than before. There I was, almost four years after I broke that man's heart, and I really expected him to be single, waiting for me to let him back into my life again? How stupid could I be?

The drive home was a blur. After arriving at my parents' house, I hurried and ran into my room before either of my parents could see me and threw myself onto my bed. Then, I cried the rest of the night like I hadn't in a long time, letting every disappointment for all my bad choices pour out onto my bed. Life was looking up for everyone I knew except me, and I just couldn't seem to find solid footing when it came to my love life.

Maybe I was just unlovable. Maybe my selfish ways had made me unappealing. There had to be a reason why love hadn't found me yet. I knew I needed to make a change but was clueless as to what to do differently. All I knew was that my heart couldn't take much more, and I needed to get it together soon or I'd be a miserable mess for the rest of my life.

CHAPTER 5

I arrived home around noon the next day. As I pulled into my parking space, I did a quick scan to make sure David was nowhere in sight. It had been a couple weeks since our sexcapade, and I had been ducking him ever since. I knew it was wrong, but David brought on a whole new set of complications that I wasn't ready for or equipped to handle. I needed to get my whole life together before I even entertained the idea of being with someone, and that included him, no matter how messed up it was. As I gazed over at David's house, I noticed a car I'd never seen before parked near his.

Hmmm, I wonder if he's seeing someone. However, I quickly forced the thought out of my mind. If David was seeing someone else, that was his business. He was not my man, and I had no business clocking who he was spending time with.

See, that's the problem, Nakia. You're always worried about the wrong thing and putting yourself in these terrible situations. You better leave that man in peace.

I didn't have to tell myself twice. I would mind my business and focus on myself and getting my mind right, because obviously I hadn't done enough self-reflection and work on myself as I thought I had. I needed to confront my issues so that I could stop self-sabotaging. I had to do everything I could to make sure I became a better me, even if that meant I had to put men on the back burner entirely and be celibate.

The next day I arrived to work bright and early, feeling rejuvenated and focused. Even my walk was different, and everyone I saw that day mentioned how I seemed to have a glow about me. It felt good to be carefree for once. I also had a review coming up with my supervisor, and I wanted to make sure everything was on point so that I could get a raise.

"Hey, Jordyn. What's up?" I asked, as I peeked into Jordyn's office on the way to mine.

"Hey, Nakia. Nothing much. How was your weekend with your parents?"

"It was cool. I spent some time with my family, linked up with an old friend, and got some closure on some unresolved issues."

"Uh oh. That sounds like man trouble to me."

"Nope. No man, and no trouble at all. Just resolution, and I honestly feel wonderful!" I said before bursting out laughing.

"Well, that's good I guess," Jordyn replied, eyeing me suspiciously. "Anyway, it's nice to see you are in such a good mood because we have a whole stack of paperwork to review for a new client. I thought I'd come by your office and we could go over everything once you were settled."

"Sure. I'm just going to put my stuff down and run and get some coffee from the break room. Meet me in my office in about ten?"

"Great. I'll be over in a bit."

After dropping off my things in my office, I headed toward the breakroom to grab some coffee. The way Jordyn was talking, I knew I was in for a busy day and would definitely need a caffeine high.

"Hey, Nakia. Can you come here? I have a message for you," Janine said.

"Sure. What's up?" I asked as I walked toward the reception desk.

"While you were out yesterday, a gentleman by the name of Mr. Amir Majid called you a few times. It seemed like it was urgent that he speak with you. He even asked for your cell or home phone number, but I couldn't give him that information. He left his number for you to call him," she said, before handing me a memo note with his name and phone number written on it.

"Thanks, Janine," I said before heading back toward the breakroom.

What in the world? What could this man possibly want? By that point, I'd totally put Amir and everything that went down between us out of my mind. So, I couldn't imagine why, so many weeks without a word from him, he would be calling me. How did he get my work number in the first place? The more I thought about it, the more pissed I became. He had some nerve. Just when I was focused on getting my life together, more drama was headed my way. I couldn't help but think I was a drama magnet. Everywhere I turned, some bullshit was happening. However, I refused to fall for it. The devil is a lie and I was determined to stay on the right path.

After grabbing my coffee, I headed back to my office to get to work with Jordyn. She was already waiting for me when I returned. Jordyn was right. We had a lot of work to do, so in order to catch up, we both decided to order in for a working lunch. By the time 5 o'clock came, I couldn't have been more ready to head home. But no matter how hard I tried, I couldn't put Amir completely out of my mind. I needed to know how he found me first of all, and most importantly, I needed to know why he thought it was okay to call me after he bounced from the hotel room that day. In fact, the whole thing bothered me so much that I pulled over on the way home and gave him a call.

The phone rang a few times, and right when I was about to hang up, he answered.

"Yeah, this is Nakia. I'm not sure what you want, nor do I really care, but I'd appreciate it if you didn't call me at my job."

"Nakia? Oh my god, I'm so glad to hear your voice. Listen, I know you may think the worst of me, but I think things got mixed up somehow. Did you get the note I left you on the nightstand in the hotel room?"

"Note? No, I didn't see any notes, Amir," I replied, rolling my eyes. I was not interested in any bullshit lies as to why he left me that morning without saying goodbye. As far as I was concerned, he had no excuse, note or not.

"Yes, I left you a note. I got a phone call while you were asleep. It was a family emergency. I didn't want to wake you, so I left you a note with my information on it asking you to call me when you woke up. When I never heard from you, I assumed you never saw the note. I've been trying to track you down ever since. Last week, I contacted the organizers of the conference and was able to get your law firm's information from them. I'm sorry. I should've handled things differently."

I wasn't sure if I should believe Amir, but he sounded sincere. Was it possible he really did leave a note and I somehow overlooked it? That wouldn't be surprising. I wasn't exactly the most patient person, and once I'd decided that he'd played me, I would've overlooked anything in my anger.

"So, what was the emergency, Amir?"

"My mom called me panicking because someone broke into the house. She was so scared, and I knew I'd be the only one to calm her down."

My anger began to dissipate. I could definitely understand how scary that must have been. I almost had a panic attack when Toni told me about her break-in.

"So, what do you want from me now, Amir? Maybe things happened the way they did for a reason," I replied in a softer tone.

"No, I don't believe that. Look, I really want to see you again, Nakia. I'm going to be in your area tomorrow for business, and I was hoping I could take you to dinner. I really just want to see you again, nothing more. I'll even pick you up from your office and drop you off there after dinner, so you know I have no other intentions."

I was silent as I contemplated whether I wanted to see Amir again. If he was telling the truth and he did leave me a note, I really had no reason to be angry. Plus, he did go through a lot to get back in touch with me. The least I could do was have dinner with him.

"Okay. I'll go to dinner with you. You can pick me up at my office around 5 tomorrow."

"Great! I'll see you then."

After we hung up, I began to wonder whether I was setting myself up for failure once again. Just when I'd made a vow of celibacy in the interest of self-care, some very good and nicely sized peen decided to pop up. Thinking about seeing Amir had me worried about what I was getting myself into. I contemplated calling Amir back and cancelling, but of course, my curiosity took over. It seemed as though my hormones were stronger than my common sense.

As I walked out of the door to my office building, I could see Amir waiting for me at the bottom of the stairs. A huge grin spread across his face once he saw me. I couldn't help but smile back as my heart raced. I'd almost forgotten how fine Amir was, and seeing him outside in the sunlight made me appreciate his looks even more.

As I neared him, he pulled me in close for an embrace. I instantly recognized his intoxicating scent, and I could already feel those familiar tingles of yearning begin to run through my body as his arms tightened around me.

"Damn, Nakia, you look amazing. I haven't stopped thinking about you since our time in New York," he said softly into my ear.

His breath brushed across my skin as he spoke. It reminded me of how his lips traveled across my body in my hotel room. My face felt warm as it rested against his muscular chest, and I couldn't ignore the bliss forming between my thighs as thoughts of our previous lovemaking filled my head.

As I stood in his embrace, the feelings flowing within me became so intense, I had to pull away from him before I did something I shouldn't have—and before someone from my office saw us.

"Is the black Lexus yours?" I asked as I gently pulled away and gestured toward the running car parked closest to us.

Then I heard a familiar voice from behind me. "Really, that's how you gonna do me, Nakia?" As I turned around in the direction of the voice, my heart skipped a beat.

"David? What are you doing here?" Suddenly, images of him and Kyle brawling at the funeral home flooded my mind. *Oh, no. What is happening?*

"Yeah, I tried to tell you she ain't shit, bro," another voice said from the other side of me. "All she does is break hearts."

I turned in the opposite direction, and was even more shocked to see Jerell, standing with his arms crossed and an expression on his face I couldn't quite read.

What the hell? This can't be real...what is happening? What are they all doing here?

As I stared at the three of them in awe, all I could hear was a cacophony of voices yelling angrily at me and each other, and as I watched the scene unfold in front of me, all I wanted to do was disappear. So, I closed my eyes and focused on a way to get out of the mess I'd gotten myself into. Then, somewhere in the distance, I heard a loud banging, followed by another voice yelling. As the voice grew closer, I began to make out what the voice was saying.

"Ma'am. Are you okay? Can you hear me?"

I felt the banging on the window, vibrating right next to me. Eventually, the voice seemed to be coming from right next to me, and I could no longer hear the others yelling. That's when I opened my eyes to find myself sitting in my car, still parked on the side of the road. A man with a concerned look on his face was banging on my window. I must have dozed off.

As I rolled down my window partially, I thought of what I'd say. I couldn't imagine how crazy I must have appeared.

"I'm good, sir. Thank you for checking on me," I said, feeling embarrassed. He nodded and walked away toward his car, and once he drove off, I turned the ignition and began driving toward my house. *Damn, these men are wearing me the hell out,* I thought as I shook my head. I couldn't remember a time that I'd fallen asleep in the car like that. That's when it became clear that I had no business meeting up with Amir. I did not want my nightmare to come true, so, I made sure to call him and cancel the moment I arrived home. No matter how sexy Amir was, my intuition told me to leave him alone. Something wasn't right about him, and I didn't want to know what it was.

CHAPTER 6

EARLY FALL

It was a cool, Saturday afternoon, and I was getting dressed to head over to Jordyn's. Over the summer our friendship had blossomed, and we had made plans to link up at her place for lunch and just chill for the day. I was happy she'd invited me because outside of work and the grocery store, I'd been stuck in the house bored, and I was tired of it. Plus, I knew the boredom of being alone would get to me eventually, and I didn't want to stay home and risk making a call I'd regret later.

Before heading to Jordyn's, I stopped at the grocery store to pick up some wine and dessert. As I headed out of the supermarket and into the parking lot, I noticed David exiting his vehicle. Luckily, my car was on the other side of the parking lot, and I quickly turned and headed towards my car, hopeful that he hadn't seen me. I knew I'd have to confront David at some point—I mean we lived in the same complex. Plus, I still felt bad about my little "hit and run" the last time I'd seen him. However, despite all of my feelings, I forced myself to believe it was best for me to keep my distance—regardless of how inevitable it was that we'd cross paths. But, as I walked up to Jordyn's front door, I had no clue how soon the inevitable would come.

"So, tell me about Adonis. How long have y'all been together?" I asked Jordyn between bites of grilled chicken salad. Adonis was Jordyn's boyfriend whom she'd mentioned every so often when we'd hung out, but he was mostly a mystery, and I was curious about the man who had stolen the heart of such a stunning young woman.

"Well, we met while I was in France, but he's American. We were working on the same shoot, and we hit it off right away. I guess what I like the most about him is how attentive he is— his affection and just the genuine care he shows for me and my dreams. He encourages and motivates me to be my best, and he supports all my decisions. Oh, and the fact that he's fine as hell doesn't hurt." We both laughed.

"Anyway, when he moved back to the States, it didn't take me long to follow him. He's actually my first serious relationship, and while there's an age difference between us, none of that seems to matter when we're together. It's like we're meant to be—shoot, he's even met my folks and everything."

"Wow, he sounds like a great guy! You're blessed. Hopefully, I can meet him someday."

"Yeah, he's amazing," she replied, cheesing.

As Jordyn and I continued to talk about our respective lives, I reminisced on my own relationships. I'd wasted so much precious time with a complete stranger, and as I looked at the young woman sitting in front of me with a promising future ahead of her, I longed to have those years back. I must have been silent for a while because my thoughts were interrupted by Jordyn.

"Hey, Nakia. You alright?"

"Yeah, I'm fine, girl. Just thinking." I forced a smile.

"Oh, okay. For a moment, you looked really sad."

"No, I'm fine. I really am. Just getting a bit of the itis I guess," I laughed. "That salad was delicious."

"Great! I'm glad you liked it. Do you want some more wine?"

Just then, a loud rumble of thunder sounded from outside, followed by a bright streak of lightning that lit up the sky. Jordyn and I were so deep in conversation, neither one of us noticed the darkening sky and the signs of a storm that was rapidly approaching. The rain began pouring.

"Oh, damn. I think I might need to head home. I had no clue it was supposed to storm today," I said as I rose from the sofa and began gathering my things.

"Oh, that's a shame! I didn't either. I wish we could hang out some more. I hate being home alone—it's so boring. Usually, me and Adonis are together on the weekends, but he's working."

"Oh, so you're just using me because your boo isn't around. I see what it is," I teased.

"No! No, not at all. I enjoy hanging out with you, and please know, you're welcome at my home anytime. I really appreciate you embracing me at work and most importantly, our friendship. To be honest, outside of Adonis, you're the only friend I have."

"Awww, I find that hard to believe. But, thank you. It was nice hanging out with you as well. We are due for some more shopping. I'm long overdue for some new clothes."

"Okay. I'll definitely take you up on that offer because I can most definitely shop!"

After saying goodbye to Jordyn, I rushed out the door and ran to my car, trying not to get drenched by the rain. As I drove toward my house, I couldn't help but think how nice it would be to go home to someone to cuddle up with. My bed had been empty for a little bit, and while sex wasn't necessarily on my mind as much, the need for companionship was. I missed the warmth of a man against my skin and the scent of a man on my sheets and pillows. I missed dinner and movie dates, and I missed being loved on. They say that it's better to be alone than lonely—but in my case I was both, and frankly, I didn't like either one.

While driving home, I noticed my car riding funny and seemingly unlevel. I was only a few blocks away from my house, and I was really hoping I would make it home with no issues. I turned down the radio to listen for any weird sounds coming from my car, but the sound of the storm was all I could hear. However, the vibration and unsteadiness I felt grew strong enough to let me know something was definitely wrong. Reluctantly, I turned on my hazards, pulled to the side of the road, grabbed the flashlight I kept in the glove compartment, and hopped out to see if I noticed anything wrong. I flashed the light across my rear driver's side when I noticed the problem. A flat tire. Just my luck.

I didn't know how to change a tire. My father had offered to teach me several times, but I always brushed him off. Typical me—never listening. Frustrated, I got back in my car and sat, trying to figure out how I'd get home. I contemplated trying to drive the rest of the way, but the tire was too flat, and I was confident I wouldn't make it without totally damaging my rim. There was no one nearby who I could call to help me, I did not have roadside assistance, and I was beginning to accept the fact I'd have to leave my car and walk in the storm. What started out as a perfectly beautiful day had turned into a nightmare, and the ominous setting from the storm raging around me made me feel even worse.

Just as I was preparing to get out and walk, I could see the lights from a car pulling up slowly through my rearview mirror. While I was leery about asking a stranger for help, I realized it was probably the only chance I'd have at not getting totally drenched on the fifteen-minute walk home. I attempted to get a glimpse of the person who was driving, but the torrential downpour blurred my vision. I rolled down my window just enough to see the passenger window of the other car as someone began rolling it down, and my heart skipped a beat as I realized who the driver was.

"Nakia, is that you?"

It was David. My face became hot, but I did my best to compose myself and hope that he'd help me out of my situation. I could only imagine how upset he was with me after I'd basically ghosted him, but now wasn't the time or the place for any of that.

"Hey. David." I took a deep breath. "Thanks for stopping. I have a flat tire—do you think you can help me?"

Wind had coupled with the rain and was making it hard to have a conversation. David must've noticed my frustration with talking through a one-inch window opening because he waved me toward the direction of his car.

"Get in, quick!" He seemed as if he was genuinely concerned, and I was relieved because I truly didn't deserve any of his kindness. I moved quickly from my car to his but still managed to get drenched. No sooner had I sat down and closed the door than the awkwardness began to set in.

"What are you doing out here in this mess?"

"I was on my way home from a friend's house."

"Hmmm ... a friend. Well, your friend doesn't seem like much of a friend if he lets you drive home alone in a storm."

"First off, who said it's a 'he'?"

"Oh, just a guess. It would make sense since you dipped out on me in the middle of the night. You are seeing someone else is the only reason I could think that anyone would do something like that. Unless the sex was lame, but based on my memories of the experience, I don't think that was the case."

"You have no idea what you're talking about. Look, the weather is bad. Would you mind just dropping me off at my house? I'll call a tow truck when I get home to bring my car to me." *I don't know who he thinks he is, but I am not his woman, and I do not owe him any explanations.*

"Look, I'm sorry. I didn't mean to come off like you owe me any explanations. I just thought we were beginning something, and when you left without saying goodbye—I'm going to be real with you—that shit hurt. Especially since I thought you and I were more than just some one-night stand type of shit."

I didn't know what to say, so I said nothing. David was absolutely right. I treated him like shit when all he'd ever been was kind to me. He was a good man, and he didn't deserve it. We sat in silence, both of us lost in our own thoughts, as the rain continued to beat down heavily on the car.

"But look, it's over and done with. I'll drive you home, and then I'll call the tow. I'll make sure they fix the tire and get the car back to you. I have roadside assistance, so it won't cost me anything."

"Thank you. I appreciate it."

We rode to my house without another word to each other, the only sound filling the air was a sports report playing on the radio. As we neared my house, I reached down for my purse to get my keys before realizing I'd left both my keys and my purse in my car.

"Shit!"

"What?" David asked as he looked over at me. He slowed to a stop in front of my house.

I waited a moment before answering.

"I left my keys and my purse in the car. I'm tired. I'm wet. I'm cold. I have to pee, and this has been the worst experience. I don't know how much more I can take." I was feeling the beginnings of a tension headache and an emotional break-down, and I'm sure David could tell from my voice. Normally, I wouldn't get so upset over something so little; however, seeing David brought out suppressed feelings that I was having a lot of trouble dealing with.

"Nakia, don't worry," David said softly. "You can wait in my house. I'll call the tow truck then head back to the car and wait for it to arrive."

I didn't say anything. I just nodded in agreement. As we entered his house, I let out a sigh of relief as warmth moved across my body.

"Can I use your bathroom?"

"Sure, go right ahead."

As I finished in the bathroom, I was impressed at how clean everything was. David was definitely not the typical bachelor I'd encountered in my life. In fact, he seemed almost perfect, and I think that was what made me nervous about him—the fear of finding out his flaws. Kyle had really messed my head up.

As I exited the bathroom and walked back into the living room, David was there waiting with a towel and a change of clothes in hand.

"They may be a little big for you, but I figured you might want to dry off and change out of those clothes."

"Thank you." I took the towel and clothing then headed back into the bathroom to change. I could hear David leave out the front door shortly afterward.

After drying off and changing into David's oversized clothes, I walked into his kitchen to search for a plastic bag to put my wet clothes in. Then, after finding one, I sat down on the couch to wait for him to return. At some point I must have fallen asleep because I awoke to a dark room and a blanket over me.

As I sat up on the couch, I could hear a running shower coming from David's bedroom. My eyes began to adjust to the darkness of the room when I noticed my purse and keys on the coffee table. The time on the stereo system read 12:12 AM, and I realized I had been sleeping for several hours. I wondered why David didn't wake me when he returned.

As if on cue, I heard the door to David's bathroom open, and I glanced in the direction of his bedroom, I caught a glimpse of him walking past in only his boxers. His body glistened with water from the shower, and his muscular body looked just as enticing as I remembered. His boxers fit snugly against him in all the right places, and a tingle traveled through my spine as I remembered the feeling of his body on top of mine. I couldn't help but think about how he'd been the last one I'd been with. As I watched him continue to dry off in the doorway, my mind dove deeper and deeper into the gutter. I needed to stop staring at that man, but before I could turn my head, he turned in my direction and caught me looking.

"Oh, hey. You're awake. I'll be right out." Then, he walked out of sight to another part of his room before coming out a few moments later wearing a t-shirt and some basketball shorts.

"Hey, I'm sorry I didn't wake you when I got home, but you looked so peaceful. I figured with the day you had, it would be best to let you rest. I honestly thought you'd wake up sooner. But everything is taken care of with your car, and it's parked in your driveway."

"Thank you. I appreciate everything."

The smell of fresh soap from David's shower flooded my nostrils as he walked closer to me, and I did my best to remain calm—however, inside, everything about David was turning me on. *Damn, he's fine.*

"Anytime. You have my number ... if you need anything, just call."

I sure the hell might.

"Well, I guess I'll get going. Sorry for ruining your evening. I'm sure you probably had plans—it is Saturday."

"Nah, no plan at all. I'm just happy I drove by when I did and I could be of some help."

"Yeah, me too. Well, I guess I'll get ready to head back home. Thanks again for everything." I grabbed my purse and keys from the coffee table then headed toward the door.

"Nakia, wait..."

I turned around to look at David. He looked back at me as if he was contemplating what he wanted to say.

"Yes?"

He sighed. "Did I do something wrong? What happened with us?"

David hung his head, and my heart dropped. I didn't know what to say—mainly because I didn't have any answer for him. I was unsure what was going on with me, but I couldn't allow David to blame himself. I also didn't know how to tell David that I was scared *because* he was so good to me.

"No, you didn't do anything wrong."

"So then, what is it? I mean, were you feeling me at all? Was I reading everything wrong?" David exhaled, as if he'd been waiting to get it all off his chest. "I guess I just thought something was developing between us." He looked into my eyes.

"I'm scared," I said, realizing how vulnerable I was allowing myself to be, but he deserved my honesty.

"You don't have to be scared of me, Nakia. I could never— would never—hurt you. All I want to do is take care of you—take care of your heart in a way that it never has never been taken care of before. I'm not the other guy who lied to you and broke your heart. I'm the guy who will pick up those pieces and mend them and make you whole again. I'm the guy who wants to penetrate you in ways more than sex ever could—I want to penetrate your mind, body, and soul, if you'll let me."

As David stared into my eyes, I knew that he meant every word. That familiar flutter began to move inside of me in response to how close his body was against mine. He was so close I could feel the heat from his body emanating from his skin onto mine.

"Can you trust me, Nakia?"

I waited a moment before whispering, "I'll try."

David smiled as he looked into my eyes a few moments longer. He lifted my chin and kissed me softly. His lips were soft and tasted like a hint of mint. He pecked me on the lips a few times before sucking on my bottom lip and letting his tongue dive in and dance with mine. He scooped me up into his arms and carried me into his bedroom. He lay me down onto his bed and slowly began to undress me. My body shivered at his touch—not because I was cold, but because I was anticipating every part of him.

He walked over to his dresser drawer and pulled out a bottle of oil. He returned moments later and poured the oil into his hands and began to massage my body, starting at my feet. Relaxation hit as my eyes closed and his strong hands finessed my skin, massaging up and down my legs. His hands occasionally traveling into the crevices of my inner thighs, his fingertips gently brushing across the lips of my yoni, before moving up to my stomach, and stopping just below my breast.

He repeated those motions several times before taking one of his fingers and gently parting my lips and moving up to my pearl. He stroked my moistened pearl with one finger, using another finger to trace the circle of my areolas as I purred softly with pleasure. Wetness spilled onto his sheets beneath me. He noticed and gently parted my legs before diving headfirst between my thighs. As he drank my juices, I arched my back and held his face in place. It wasn't long before I felt a familiar buzz of an orgasm forming below as the lovemaking he was performing with his mouth became more intense.

As the passion within me grew, I fidgeted on the bed. My legs trembled, and my moans got louder. This seemed to turn him on even more. He stood up, slipped off his clothes, and climbed on top of me. He was at full attention, and all I wanted was to feel him inside me. He kissed me softly, and I could taste the remnants of my sweet juices on his lips. We kissed passionately as his hardness teased the opening of my core. He entered me slowly, and I whimpered as I took in every inch of him. He felt so good I could cry. I spread my legs even more before grabbing his ass and guided him deeper inside of me. As his strokes went deeper and faster, my toes curled from the ecstasy.

"Damn, I missed you Nakia," he moaned.

"I missed you too."

He made sure my body was pleasured everywhere. His attentiveness was what I needed, and after what felt like hours of pure bliss, we both climaxed then retired into each other's arms, completely spent. I fell into a deep sleep that I didn't wake from until early afternoon. As I awoke the next day in David's bed, I internally scolded myself for not staying the last time I was there. I shook my head at what I'd made the mistake of giving up all those weeks ago, but made a vow to myself that I'd stop being so guarded and let David care for me the way he said he would.

CHAPTER 7

It was a little over a month later and this "thing" David and I were in was going pretty well. While we hadn't exactly made it official, I decided to just go with the flow and see how things would turn out. I had tried my best to be single and free after the divorce, and I was miserable the whole time. At least with what David and I had, I wasn't lonely, and it didn't hurt that I was getting piped down on the regular either.

However, it didn't take me long to realize it was more than sex for David. I knew his feelings were growing for me quickly by the things he said. I even suspected that he might be in love with me, but at the moment, I think I was more in love with the sex than anything else—and thinking about it too long made me nervous, so I tried to keep my focus on just having fun. But I couldn't deny David was amazing, and I regretted not allowing myself to enjoy all that he was offering me much earlier. Especially since he was proving that he was a great guy.

Despite how well things were going, however, I still anticipated that his flaws would eventually reveal themselves. The ugly side of him would have to show up sooner or later if it existed, so I did remain at least slightly guarded. After all, I was still a work in progress and looked forward to the day that I could completely surrender myself to him emotionally.

One evening after having dinner at his place, we were cuddled up on the sofa watching a movie when he got a phone call. It was his mother. As I continued to watch the movie, I half listened in on their conversation.

"Hey, Mama. How have you been feeling? Have you been taking your medicine?

You sure? Okay, I believe you. I was just making sure. I don't want you back in that hospital... Oh, nothing, much—just sitting here with Nakia, watching a movie. Yes, you'll get to meet her ... Soon ... I promise ... Okay, Mama. You can come by tomorrow... Yes, around noon. I'll make lunch ... Okay. We'll see you tomorrow ... I love you too."

I wanted to pretend I wasn't paying attention to his conversation, but I was feeling a little annoyed about David making plans for me to meet his mother without even consulting me.

Like, how did he know I didn't have any plans of my own? How did he know I was ready for that step? As far as I was concerned, we were just having fun, and I was pissed that he was trying to make things complicated so early on. I knew nothing about his mother, and I wasn't really in the mood for making impressions.

In fact, while things were good between us, I felt like spending every free moment together was unhealthy. I can't count how many times David had canceled plans with his boys to spend time with me without me asking him to and then expected me do the same with my friends. I liked being with him, but I was starting to get a sense of his clingy nature. I just didn't know how to tell him without hurting his feelings.

"What did I miss?" David asked as he snuggled back in close to me after hanging up with his mother.

"I don't know, David. Maybe try the rewind button." I probably shouldn't have said it in that tone or used those words, but I was extremely annoyed with him.

"Okkkkay." David was silent for a moment, but I could tell he was surprised by my tone. He sat up on the couch, which required me to readjust as well because of how we were positioned. "What's wrong?" He looked over at me, worry filling his eyes.

"Nothing." I redirected my gaze, refusing to look at him.

"There's obviously something wrong. I can tell by your tone and your body language. Just tell me what's up. We were just chilling a few moments ago and then my mama ca ... Oh. My mom. Are you upset with me because I made plans for you to meet my mother, Nakia?"

I didn't answer.

"Babe, I'm sorry. You have every reason to be upset with me. I should've asked you first, but if it makes you feel better, I've told my mom all about you, and she's just anxious to meet the woman who has made me so happy lately. My mother has actually known about you since you were married to Kyle. She's been wanting to meet you since then, but it never happened for obvious reasons."

"Wait a minute. You told your mom about me, a married woman, spending her free time with a single man while her husband was in prison? Really? I can only imagine what kind of woman she thinks I am!" I was no longer simply annoyed, I was pissed! Who did David think he was? No woman of David's mother's age would condone such a relationship, and while David and I never had sex while I was with Kyle, I could guarantee that's not what his mother thought. She probably thought I was some kind of whore trying to trap her son. That's why she was so insistent on meeting me. *What the hell, David?* Why did he have to go and mess up a good thing?

David took a deep breath, then stayed silent for a moment, as if he were picking his words carefully.

"I just thought that with everything that's happening between us, meeting each other's parents would be the logical next step in our relationship."

"Relationship? What relationship? David, we're spending time together and having sex—that's it. I've never committed to a relationship with you. I told you I was open to see where things would go, but I NEVER agreed that I was yours exclusively."

"Wait? So, are you saying you've been with other men while we've been together? Are you serious? We don't even use condoms half the time. I know you're not out here messing around with other men at the same time you've been fooling around with me."

I didn't answer him. I just turned my head. The truth was, I couldn't be with another man if I wanted to since all my time was spent at either work or with him. But, if he wanted to be foolish and not realize that fact, I wasn't going to try to change his mind.

"Wow. That's great, Nakia. I don't know why I thought more of you." Without another word, he rose from the sofa, walked into his bedroom, and closed the door. I took it as my cue to leave, so I grabbed my things and left. While a part of me knew I was wrong, another part of me wanted a break from David, so I allowed my stubbornness to direct my ass home.

CHAPTER 8

It was a Friday night, almost a week after I'd seen or talked to David, and I was sitting in the house, bored. He'd called me several times and left many messages apologizing and asking me to call him, but I ignored his calls. I just wasn't ready to deal with him. My heart wanted to be with him, but my head was just so messed up. I couldn't give him what he needed emotionally. I enjoyed spending time with David, he treated me well, and the sex was amazing. But I really needed to take my time with my next relationship, and he wanted things to move at a faster pace than I was ready for.

As I sat thinking about everything that was going on with David and me, my phone rang. It was Jordyn.

"Hey, girl. What's up?"

"Hey, Nakia. Are you busy?" I wasn't sure, but it sounded as if she'd been crying.

"No, not at all. What's wrong Jordyn?"

There was a pause and could hear her sniffling.

"Nakia—I'm pregnant. I don't know what I'm going to do."

I didn't know what to say. Honestly, the way Jordyn seemed so in love, I wasn't sure why she was upset.

"Do you think you can come over? I just need someone to talk to."

"Oh, okay. Sure, Jordyn. I'll be there in about a half hour."

"Okay. Thanks, Nakia. I appreciate it."

"No problem. I'll see you soon."

After hanging up, I quickly threw on some clothes, then grabbed my keys to head out to Jordyn's. As I approached my car, I glanced down the street to David's house. His car was in the driveway, but all the lights were off. I couldn't lie—I missed him—but that was not enough to make me call him back.

I arrived at Jordyn's house about twenty minutes later. After settling down in her living room, I took in Jordyn's appearance. She was dressed casually in a t-shirt and some sweatpants, but her hair wasn't done, and her eyes were red and puffy.

"I know you're probably wondering why I'm upset about being pregnant, but once I tell you the whole story, I think you'll understand."

"Okay."

"First off, promise you won't judge me after you hear what I have to say."

"Girl, I doubt there's anything you can do to make me think less of you. I've had my share of fuck ups."

"Okay. Well, lately, I've been feeling really nauseous, and I've had a crazy appetite. I've also noticed I've been gaining weight in my stomach, and my period hasn't come in more than two months. At first, I tried to ignore it, but once the nausea started, I realized I needed to take a pregnancy test. So, a few days ago, I went to the doctor's and had one done. I got the results yesterday. I'm definitely pregnant."

"Okay. Did you tell your boyfriend? Or are you worried about what he'll think?"

"No, I didn't tell him."

"Why not, Jordyn?"

Jordyn paused as if thinking about whether she should say more. Then, as if she decided that she would tell me, she quickly blurted, "It's not his."

My mouth dropped open in awe. I didn't know what to say, but I didn't want Jordyn to think I thought badly of her, so I quickly fixed my face and tried to compose myself.

"Do you know whose it is?" I asked carefully.

"Yeah ... it's Brad's."

Brad ... who is Brad? Wait ... Brad?

"Jordyn, are you talking about Brad? White boy Brad from HR at work?"

"Yes," Jordyn said softly before hanging her head in shame.

"Wait—I guess I'm confused as to how this happened. I mean I know *how* it happened, but I guess what I'm trying to say is that I didn't know you two were messing around."

"It only happened a few times. I don't know why I did it. I guess I haven't really been with anyone else other than Jerell, and I was kind of curious about how it would be with someone new. I'm still young, and I wanted to expose myself to more than one person sexually, but I also didn't want to hurt Jerell."

"Jerell?" I felt sick to my stomach. Everything was beginning to click, and I wasn't liking it. *My* Jerell had a new girlfriend and therefore wasn't interested in revisiting a relationship with me. Meanwhile, Jordyn's boyfriend was a model who she met in France. What were the odds? No, this couldn't be. Maybe it was just one big coincidence. Jordyn's boyfriend couldn't be MY ex, Jerell.

"Jordyn, I thought your boyfriend's name was Adonis?"

"Yeah, that's his model name, and that's what I call him most of the time, but his real name is Jerell."

I didn't say anything to Jordyn about my suspicions. I wasn't exactly sure if she was dating *my* Jerell, so, instead of bringing it up, I redirected the conversation to Brad.

"So, what are you going to do? Are you going to tell Brad? Also, how do you know it's not Jerell's? I know you slept with Brad, but how do you know for sure which one is the father?"

"I just know. The timing adds up with Brad, and Jerell and I haven't been intimate in a while. That's another reason why I've been messing around with Brad. I've honestly been horny, and Jerell has seemed distracted lately."

My heart was beating rapidly in my chest, and I realized Jordyn wasn't the only one feeling sick. My face was hot, and I knew I needed to get myself under control quickly.

"Jordyn, can I use your bathroom?"

"Sure, just walk straight to the back of the hall," she replied, pointing to the right.

I had barely made it to the bathroom before I began hyperventilating. It seemed like drama followed me wherever I went. After splashing my face with water and catching my breath, I realized I needed to get out of there. While I felt sorry for Jordyn, I knew I wouldn't be of any help to her, so I quickly came up with an excuse as to why I had to leave and then exited the bathroom. But before I joined Jordyn back in the living room, I quickly tiptoed into the bedroom next door, hoping I'd see a picture of her and her boo. I wanted to confirm whether or not it was the same Jerell. I didn't have to walk far before getting a glimpse of a huge portrait on the wall above her bed of the couple. My worst fears were confirmed. It was *my* Jerell. After gathering myself once again, I tiptoed out of Jordyn's bedroom and then hurried back down the hall to join her in her living room. My mind was a wreck. In what world was the girl I'd become friends with at work my ex's new girlfriend?

"Hey, Jordyn. I'm not sure what's wrong, maybe it's something I ate, but I'm not feeling well either. I'm sorry, but I have to head home."

"Oh, okay. I understand. Let me walk you to the door." Jordyn looked sad that I was leaving so soon, but I really needed to be alone in the privacy of my own house. After giving Jordyn a hug and some reassuring words that I believed everything would be alright, I told her I'd call her when I got home, then I headed to my car.

As I pulled away from Jordyn's place, I was literally shaking. I didn't know why Jerell was still affecting me the way that he was, but I was starting to think my unresolved feelings for him were stopping me from a future with David. It was like a part of me still believed that Jerell was the one who got away. Now that I knew that Jerell was Jordyn's man, I started to doubt I'd be able to remain her friend, and I hated feeling that way.

After I got home, I took a long bath, changed into my pajamas, and grabbed a container of rum raisin ice cream that I'd been saving for what I called a "Lifetime moment"—a moment where I could just curl up on my couch, watch Lifetime movies, and cry. I felt horrible, my life was going down the drain, and once again I'd found myself alone. To top it all off, I was horny as hell and was doing my best to resist my urge to call David.

Somewhere in between eating ice cream and bawling my eyes out, I must have fallen asleep, because I awoke a few hours later to my phone ringing. I glanced at the caller ID only to find out the number was "Unknown." Against my better judgment, I answered.

"Hello?"

"Nakia?"

"Who's this?" I asked suspiciously. It was 11 at night, and there was no reason for anyone I didn't know to be calling me. Shit ... people I did know barely called me that late.

"Amir."

I sat up on the couch. *Why is he calling me? What could he possibly want to talk about at this time of night?*

"Yes?"

"Hey. I'm sorry I'm calling so late. I've just been thinking about you, and I know you told me the last time we talked that nothing could happen between us, but I'm not one to give up so easily. I also need to let you know how I feel ... I'm going to be real; I've been wanting you ever since the last time we were together. I miss you, Nakia."

I sighed. "Amir we barely know each other. How can you possibly miss me?"

"Well, I wouldn't say we *barely* know each other. I mean I know we've only spent those few days together in New York, but during that time I shared a lot with you, and I thought you shared a lot with me."

I sighed again. Amir and I had shared a lot about ourselves while we were together—at least in between sex sessions. Maybe I needed someone new to focus on. Both David and Jerell were men I had history with, but there was something mysterious about Amir, and I couldn't deny our sexual compatibility.

"So, what do you want from me Amir?"

"Can I see you?"

"When?"

"Now?"

"What do you mean now? Don't you live in Virginia?"

"Yes, but I had a meeting with a new client not too far from you that ended late, so I decided to stay in town and get a room. I've been working up the nerve to call you with the hopes that I'd get to see you ever since I checked in."

Life was definitely throwing me curveballs, and I didn't know how to react. All the twists and turns I'd been experiencing over the past couple of months and even weeks was a lot, and I was starting to think I was being tested. But, test or not, a girl has needs, and Amir was definitely someone who could fulfill them.

"Okay. You can come over."

After giving Amir my address, I rushed into the shower to clean up, then threw on a silk negligee and a robe. I had just finished tidying up when I heard a car pull into my driveway. A few moments later, my doorbell rang.

After taking a quick glimpse of myself in my hallway mirror, I opened the door to a grinning Amir.

"Hey, gorgeous," he beamed.

After walking in and closing the door behind himself, he pulled me in close to him for a long passionate kiss. I was instantly turned on. Amir wasted no time. No more than five minutes later, both Amir and I had undressed. After looking my body up and down, Amir licked his lips, then turned me around and pinned me against my living room wall. I loved how he took control. He reached down to pick up his pants from the floor, pulled a condom from one of the pockets, and began to slide it on. Just as he we were about to resume our activities, my phone rang.

I ignored it, hoping whoever it was would just hang up. No such luck. I'd forgotten to turn off my answering machine, and just as Amir was preparing to enter me from behind, I heard David's voice coming from my answering machine.

"Nakiaaa ... Nakiaaaa ... Are you there? Look ... I really ... really need to talktoyouuu." He was breathing heavily. *"I'm just gonna come over... I know you're there."*

"Shit!" I didn't know what was going on, but it sounded as if David was drunk, and based on his message, I was pretty sure he'd be at my door any minute. A feeling of deja vu came over me, and I remembered my dream with David, Amir, and Jerell. Then I remembered David's fight with Kyle, and I knew I had to get Amir out of there ASAP!

"Look, you have to go!"

Amir just stood there, fully erect with a slightly confused look on his face as if he was unsure whether or not I was kidding. If the situation wasn't so serious, it would actually have been quite comical. After a few moments, however, Amir realized I was serious because his expression changed.

"You can't be serious. If you have a man, why am I here?"

"I don't have a man ... look, it's complicated, and I really don't have time to explain it right now. But I don't want any mess jumping off here, so you really need to leave, and preferably through the back door."

Amir began putting on his clothes. I put on mine as well. After giving me the most pissed off look I'd ever seen, he grabbed his keys and began heading for my front door.

"Wait, Amir. I need you to go out the back," I said as nicely as I could.

Amir sucked his teeth, "Man, I don't know what you have going on, but I am NOT sneaking out of your house, so, you're just going to have to deal with whatever consequences come your way if your *man* sees me."

Before I could say another word, Amir opened my front door, and to my horror, David was standing right there. They both stood in my doorway staring at each other, and for a moment, it was almost as if they knew each other.

Then, Amir turned around to look at me, a slight grin on his face. "Wow!" he said, shaking his head. He turned back around, walked around David, jumped into his car, and sped off.

Incredulity and heartbreak were written all over David's face. "Look, David. Come in the house. Let's talk ... I can explain," I said quickly.

David just stood in my doorway as if he didn't hear me. Then, finally putting everything together in his head, his speechlessness turned to anger.

"So, you really *have* been fuckin' with someone else?"

"No, David. I haven't. Look, just come in the house, and we can talk."

"Nah, I'm good Nakia. I should've known better. I should've known you weren't the one. Who was I fooling?"

I felt bad. I never had any intentions of hurting David, and once again, I let lust cloud my judgment. What was I thinking by having another man in my house when the man who I'd been dating for the past couple of months lived a couple of houses down from me? I needed to explain myself. I needed to make things right.

As I walked toward the doorway to try to get David to come in to talk, the strong smell of liquor filled the air.

"David, why are you drunk? What's wrong? You never drink," I said, concerned.

In all the time I'd known David, he'd never been one to drink, so it was a surprise to see him damn near pissy drunk, struggling to steady himself in my doorway.

He collapsed onto the floor of my entryway and began crying. I didn't know what to say or do. I honestly didn't know how things went from me about to get my back blown out by Amir to trying to coax a drunken David into my house to talk. What universe was I living in?

"David, what's wrong?" I asked softly.

"My mother was in a car accident. It's bad, Nakia. She's in an induced coma, and I honestly didn't have anyone else to talk to." Tears fell from his eyes as he struggled to speak. "I came home to grab some clothes before heading back to be with her, and it was all just too much, so I started drinking. I just needed someone— someone to talk to—and then I come over here to find you— with—" David stood up. "No matter what happened between us, I would never think I couldn't come to you if I needed you. But instead, I come to you for your support, and I find you with another man? Damn, Nakia! I can't believe you!"

I tried to hug David to comfort him, but he pushed me away.

"Nah, I'm good. I don't want no man's sloppy seconds. You don't have to worry about me bothering you again. I'm out. Have a good life."

Without another word, David turned around and stumbled back toward his house. All I could do was close the door behind him, then head to my bed, totally confused about everything that had happened. *This can't be my life.*

The next day, I called David several times, but he didn't answer. I couldn't be mad though. I'm sure, as far as he was concerned, I was basically getting a dose of my own medicine. Still, I wanted to apologize to David and let him know that I hadn't actually slept with Amir—at least I hadn't that night. But ultimately, I knew that none of that really mattered; if he hadn't interrupted us, we would've definitely ended up sleeping together, and I'm sure David knew that as well.

As I laid in bed, trying to get over all that had transpired, my telephone rang. It was Toni.

I did my best to sound upbeat. I didn't want her to know all the drama that had been going on with me. She would have surely called me a little ho. Plus, I knew she was probably calling me because her project at work was finished, and she was ready to start wedding planning. I didn't want to sour the mood.

"Hey, T. What's up?"

"Hey, Nakia. Nothing much, what are you doing?"

"Nothing, girl. Just sitting here watching TV."

"Oh, okay. Well, I was calling because I wanted to let you know that I'm having a dinner this Saturday at my house, and I know it's short notice, but can you come? I want you to meet AJ and his family."

"Yeah, I can come. I can actually come on Friday night, that way I can help you prepare." I was actually relieved I had an excuse to leave town for a few days. I needed to get away and heading home to Virginia was the perfect escape.

"That's great, because I'm nowhere near as good a cook as you are, and I want to impress AJ's mom."

"No problem, girl. You know I'll be there. It'll be nice to see you, and I'm looking forward to meeting my soon-to-be brother-in-law."

After catching up with Toni, I fixed myself something to eat before taking a long bath in an attempt to relax. I nervously prepared for work the next day. I had a feeling I was about to have a long week ahead of me, and all I could think of was my trip back home on Friday. I couldn't wait.

CHAPTER 9

The next morning at the office, I realized that Jordyn hadn't come into work. I felt bad that I wasn't there for her when she needed me. Regardless of her relationship with Jerell, I truly had no reason to be upset with her, so I made a mental note to call her to check on her during my lunch break. I also gave Brad the mean mug every time I saw him. I had no doubt in my mind that he'd unethically used his influence to seduce Jordyn, and I was pissed. Everyone in the office knew Brad was a sleazeball. I just wished I'd taken the time to school Jordyn on who she should and shouldn't interact with at the office. I couldn't help but feel as though I'd let her down.

At lunch, I called Jordyn, but she didn't answer. I left a voice message for her to call me back when she got a chance, then I got back to work. Later that afternoon, as I was heading to the ladies' room, I overheard the receptionist talking to one of my co-workers.

"Well, Jordyn is no longer with us."

"Wow. She's out already? She hasn't even been working here that long."

"Yeah, from what I heard, she got into a dispute with someone in HR, and the next thing anyone knew, she had submitted her resignation, effective immediately."

"Damn, I wonder who she had the dispute with."

"Well, you didn't hear it from me, but word is, she has some kind of drama going on with Brad."

"Oh, okay. Say no more. If it has to do with Brad's ho ass, I can only imagine."

I quickly walked into the bathroom before anyone noticed me eavesdropping. Damn. My girl had quit, and now she wasn't even answering the phone. I could only imagine how helpless Jordyn was feeling. I decided I'd stop by her house after work to check on her and make sure she was alright. I could relate to being young and pregnant and not having anyone to turn to. I needed to put my feelings for Jerell aside and be the friend I was supposed to be to. She needed me.

As soon as I got out of work, I headed over to Jordyn's house. I didn't know her state of mind, and I wanted to make sure she was alright. She didn't have a car, so I knew she was home most of the time when she wasn't at work. But, as I knocked on her door for several minutes with no response, I grew even more concerned. I also had no way of knowing if she was in the house and just not answering or if she wasn't at home at all. I only knew one person who might know where she was, but that was complicated. There was no way I could call Jerell to see if Jordyn was okay. He didn't even know I knew Jordyn. Or did he?

Thankfully, the rest of the week flew by, and before I knew it, I was back in Richmond. Before heading over to Toni's house, I stopped by the liquor store to pick up some wine. I was looking forward to a chill evening sipping wine and helping Toni prepare for her dinner party. Most of all, I was happy to be away from all the drama that I knew would be waiting for me when I got back home.

As I walked through the aisles to select my wine, a familiar voice called my name from behind me. I turned around to see Kyle walking toward me.

I took a deep breath. I knew since Kyle and I were from the same city that we'd eventually bump into each other.

"Hey, Kyle. How have you been?" I tried to be calm even though it felt extremely awkward between us.

"I'm okay. Same ole, same ole. Just work and home. I don't really get out too much these days, but then again, I always preferred it at home anyway."

Funny, you were barely home with me.

"Yeah, I feel you. I guess we're getting older."

"Yeah, older and wiser. Speaking of—I know you're probably over me and everything, but I just want you to know how much you've meant to me—then and now. I made a lot of mistakes with you, and I'm paying for those mistakes by not being with you, but I just wanted to let you know, you've made a major difference in my life. I can't even date anyone else because I'm always comparing them to you."

"Don't do that Kyle. Don't compare anyone new to me. It's not fair to them, and it's not fair to you either, because you'll never find someone else who is exactly like me."

"I know—which is why I'd rather find you again."

I could feel the awkwardness building up.

"So, how's Kyle Jr.?" I asked, changing the subject.

Kyle smiled. He knew what I was doing. "He's good. He lives with me now actually."

"Oh, really? Why?"

"One day, while he was at my house for the weekend, his mother called and asked me to keep him indefinitely. I was shocked but, of course, accepted the responsibility. She has a lot going on in her life, and between you and me, I think there is a bit of mental instability there."

"Oh, wow, raising a kid on your own is a big deal." A pang of sadness ripped through my heart. I thought about our baby who should've been with us. That was one thing that I had never been able to get over, no matter how hard I tried to force the experience of miscarrying out of my mind.

"You're thinking about our baby, aren't you?" Kyle was always able to read my mind. It was scary how similar we were. I just tended to be more responsible and honest—at least when I was with him, I was.

"Well, Kyle. I have to get ready to go. But it was nice seeing you. Please tell Kyle Jr. and your father I said hi." I didn't want to talk to Kyle about our child. I still hadn't forgiven him for not being there with me.

"Nice seeing you too, Nakia. I will," Kyle responded sadly before turning and walking away.

As I drove to Toni's house, I thought about how much things had changed between the first time I met Kyle and now. Our entire relationship was a whirlwind. We were like two storms combined that caused everything within and outside of our storm to collapse. If I was honest with myself, the only calm that existed was before we met, and whether Kyle wanted to admit it or not, he knew things were better when we were apart. The peace that filled me once the divorce was final let me know that much.

However, I couldn't help but eat my words to Kyle in the liquor store. How could I tell Kyle not to compare anyone new to me when I'd been comparing everyone to Jerell? At that moment I realized I'd been using Jerell as a guide on how others should treat me, when I should've just stayed my ass with Jerell in the first place. I had a lot to figure out, but for the weekend, I wanted to try to focus on Toni and making her dinner a success.

"Heyyy, girl!" I said, smiling as Toni opened the door.

"Heyyy, Nakia!" she greeted me before giving me a tight hug.

"I bought some wine—for now—not tomorrow. After the last couple of weeks I've had, I need some."

"Oh, yeah. Well, let's drink some wine then!"

We both laughed, then headed to the kitchen.

"So, what's up Nakia? Why have you been having a tough couple of weeks? And why am I just now hearing about it?" Toni asked as we settled in her living room with our wine glasses.

"Girl, why? Shoot, I wish I knew why. I don't know, T. It's like everything has just been going wrong. I thought once my divorce with Kyle was complete, my life would regain some sense of normalcy. But to be honest, after we got back from Europe, everything just went haywire. My love life and sex life are crazy, and I just don't know what to do with myself. I've been making all the wrong choices."

"So, I guess I'm missing some things, because last I heard, you had no love life," Toni teased. "I'm pretty sure the last time we talked about your love life was when you were in New York, and you told me that you weren't interested in finding love. Let me guess—you done picked back up with that almost-fling of yours from when you were still with Kyle?"

I avoided Toni's glance. I hadn't told Toni anything about what happened after we spoke on the phone in New York. She didn't know about my sexcapade with Amir at the hotel, my interaction with Jerell, or my ongoing situation with David. It wasn't like I didn't trust her with the information, I just didn't want her to judge me. Not that she would have—but when it comes to me acting a damn fool, I tend to keep it to myself.

"Yeah, there's a lot going on, but that's not what I'm here for. I'm here to support you! So, when will I meet your hubby? Is he coming over?"

"Oh, no. You're not getting away with that so easy. We're coming back to these secrets you've been keeping from me."

"Yes, I know. We'll talk about it—just not now, okay?"

"Okay. But, yeah. You'll meet AJ this weekend. He should be getting in from a business trip tonight. He'll be over right before the dinner tomorrow with his parents and his sister."

"Okay, cool. I'm excited. So tell me more about AJ. Is he from this area?"

"No, actually he's from Los Angeles. His mother flew down last week, and she's staying at his place. We met through a mutual friend, and everything just vibed between us. The chemistry is there, he looks good, the sex is amazing, he treats me well, and he's financially secure. Sometimes I think he's too perfect."

"Oh, wow. He sounds like a good guy. What does he do for a living?"

"He's a lawyer. He's older than us, but he doesn't act like it. And to be honest, I was tired of guys our age. They don't know what the hell they're doing."

"You can say that again. I used to tell you older was the way to go when you used to tease me about Jerell."

"Yeah, but then you left Jerell for Kyle."

I rolled my eyes. "Watch it, Toni," I teased.

We laughed.

"But speaking of—I just saw Kyle at the liquor store before coming to your place."

"Oh, yeah? Did you two speak?"

"Yeah. Briefly. I found out he has custody of Kyle Jr. now. He's a full-time father."

"Yeah, I've seen him and little man around a few times. We've only said as much as hello to each other though. I still think he's an asshole for how he treated you, so I don't have time to fake like I like his ass."

We both fell over laughing. That's one thing I loved about Toni—her honesty.

After we had stuffed ourselves with food and drank way too much wine, we began planning the menu for the next evening. As we were working on the menu, Toni got a phone call. It was AJ.

"Hey, babe. Did you just land? Oh, okay. Great! How was your flight? ... Yeah ... I miss you too...," she giggled. "Whatever, Amir. Stop being fresh ...."

AMIR? What the fuck! Please tell me I didn't just hear Toni say Amir? Does AJ somehow stand for Amir? Okay, maybe it's another Amir. But then again, it wasn't another Jerell. Oh my god. Please don't let this man be who I think he is.

After Toni hung up the phone, I did my best to try to appear unbothered. I didn't want her to suspect something was wrong, but inside, I was cringing at the thought that I'd possibly slept with Toni's fiancé. I mean I realized that if I had, it wasn't intentional, but it would make her man out to be a cheater, and I didn't want my best friend to be hurt. So, I played it cool and continued working on the menu for the next day. However, I knew I had to find out for sure if Toni's Amir was the same Amir I had gotten down and dirty with.

"So, all this talk about your boo, and you haven't shown me one picture," I said teasingly.

"Oh, wow. I never even thought of it. Hold on for a second, I'll go get one from my purse."

While Toni was in the other room, my heart began to beat rapidly. I really hoped that Amir wasn't a sleazeball. It would break her heart. A few moments later, Toni came in the room with a picture. As she handed me the picture and I took in the smiling couple who, for anyone else, would appear to be the perfect couple, I had to do my best to contain the anger rising inside of me. It was Amir, and I wanted to kill him!

Later that night, while Toni was asleep, I laid restless in bed. All the signs were there, and I was either too blind or too horny to see them. Amir didn't leave the hotel because of his mother's house being broken into. It was Toni's house! Then I realized there was no way he hadn't put two and two together and figured out Toni and I were friends. That's when I knew I needed to confront him. After walking past Toni's room to make sure she was sleep, I returned to the guest bedroom and quietly called Amir on my cell phone. He answered after a few rings, and he sounded surprised to hear from me.

"Nakia?"

"Yeah, it's me. Look, I don't have time to spare—I need answers. Are you engaged to a woman named Toni?"

Silence.

"Hello? Are you there, Amir?"

"Yeah ... I'm here."

"Are you going to answer my question?"

After a few moments, he responded. "Yes, my fiancée's name is Toni."

"So, you cheated on your fiancée several times with me at the hotel in New York and attempted to cheat on her the other night when you were at my house. Am I right?" My body temperature was on the rise as I wiped away the sweat beads forming on my nose.

"Yes. You're right. I made a mistake though."

"Mistake my ass. Amir, please tell me you didn't know that I was Toni's best friend...," My hands were clammy, and my heart was racing.

Silence.

"I didn't know right away. I only figured it out yesterday when Toni told me her best friend, Nakia, was coming up from Maryland for the dinner. I swear I would've never done something like this intentionally."

"Well, whether you knew I was her best friend or not, you still *intentionally* cheated on her. You're a piece of shit, and you are definitely not worthy of having MY best friend as your wife. So, are you going to tell her, or am I?"

"Nakia, I suggest you leave this shit alone. I said I made a mistake. We are going to keep this between us, and that it that." His tone changed as he was making demands.

"Keep it between us? You must be out of your goddamn mind. I can't keep something like this from her. I'm her best friend. If she ever found out, she'd never talk to me again." I felt horrible that I had unknowingly betrayed my best friend. How the hell could I explain this mess to her?

"Listen, bitch, you're not going to ruin my relationship because you wanted to be a whore and spread your legs for the first man who hit on you at a bar! I'm not telling Toni shit. And you better not say anything either—or there will be problems for you!"

"You must have me all the way fucked up. I'm a grown ass SINGLE woman, and if I want to sleep with someone the same night I meet them, that's MY business. Men do things like that all the time. Second, I don't know who you think you are, but you do NOT scare me, so keep your weak ass threats to yourself or there will be problems for YOU. Now, like I said—are you going to tell her, or should I?"

Click.

No, he didn't hang up on me. I can't believe this.

The rest of the night, I tossed and turned. It was obvious it would be up to me to tell Toni about her cheating ass man. I just hoped that it wouldn't hurt our friendship. I wished I could turn back time and erase everything that happened between Amir and me, but the truth was, Amir was a cheater, and if it wasn't me, it would've been someone else. Toni would've possibly never known and ended up making the biggest mistake of her life by marrying him. *God, why am I always involved in something crazy?* I had never felt so much anxiety in my life. By the time I fell asleep, the sun was already rising.

"Why didn't you tell me? You're my best friend! Why didn't you tell me? Huh, Nakia?"

Confused, I opened my eyes to a very angry Toni standing at the side of the bed screaming at me.

Oh, no. This is exactly what I feared. I took a deep breath. "Toni—I thought it was best that Amir tell you. I told him last night that if he didn't, I would."

"That's not what he said. He told me you asked him to keep it a secret and that he was so guilty about what he'd done, he had to tell me before we were all together at dinner tonight. How could you keep something like this from me?"

"Huh? Toni, I just found out last night when you showed me his picture!"

"Well, that's not what AJ said. He said he found out a few weeks ago when he was going through my photo album and saw a picture of the two of us. He said he immediately told you once he knew, and you begged him to keep it a secret! He even said that you tried to sleep with him AFTER you found out I was his fiancée. How could you, Nakia?" Toni slumped down on the floor. At this point she was sobbing.

Wow! I can't believe this man. I climbed out of bed and attempted to put my hand on Toni's shoulder to comfort her, but she pushed it away. "Don't touch me, bitch! I can't believe you'd want to keep something like this from me! And then come to my house and help plan for this party like there was nothing wrong. What kind of friend are you?"

"Toni, I KNOW you don't believe what this man is saying. How long have we known each other? We don't keep secrets from each other. I would never tell Amir not to tell you, and I definitely wouldn't try to sleep with him after I knew he was your man! I swear, I only found out last night!"

"Hmmm, well you never told me about your rendezvous at the hotel, so apparently you DO keep secrets from me, Nakia."

I couldn't help but think to myself that Toni had a point. There were plenty of secrets I kept from her, but it wasn't because I didn't trust her. I felt bad that she didn't think I cherished our friendship enough to share things with her. I told her mostly everything, but no one tells anyone everything. I was sure there were things I didn't know about her.

"Toni, it wasn't like that at all. If you just listen to the whole story, you'll—-"

"Get the hell out, Nakia. I can't do this. I don't want to talk to you or Amir. Leave."

"Please, Toni. Just lis—-"

"GO, NAKIA! Before I put my hands on you!"

I was shocked. As long as Toni and I had been friends, we'd never once had an argument. How could Toni believe Amir over me? Sure, I never told her about meeting someone at the hotel and sleeping with him, but that was mainly because I was embarrassed. I also didn't think anything would progress between Amir and me, so I basically tried to erase him from my mind. But I didn't want to upset Toni any more than she already was, so I quietly got my things and left. I figured she'd call me once she had some time to think. However, two weeks went by, and I still hadn't heard from her.

CHAPTER 10

LATE FALL

After I left Toni's house that day, things never quite felt right. I missed my best friend, and my love life was a hot mess. I was completely alone. I was hopeful that Toni would call, but she never did. I was too worried about upsetting her to call her as well. I hadn't heard from David either. With every day that passed, I considered calling him but didn't know what to say or how to explain myself. The loneliness gave me a lot of time to think about my actions. I was growing tired of *the single life*. I missed David and needed his presence in my life for the long term.

Jordyn eventually returned to work. Apparently, she'd never resigned, and it was all a rumor. She'd simply taken off for medical reasons. We were still friends, but I kept my distance from her as much as I could. I'd also decided not to tell her that Jerell was my ex. I honestly didn't feel like she needed to know since there was nothing going on between Jerell and me. However, I did feel bad that she was leading Jerell on and making him think she was carrying his baby when it may not have been his. As much as it hurt me to keep something so significant from a man I cared for, I decided to keep the information to myself. It was none of my business, and I was too stressed over my own problems to worry about Jerell's. On top of that, I did not want to be "that girl". The girl whose advances were denied so she dangled hurtful information in a man's his face to try to win him back.

It was the start of the weekend, and I had just arrived home from work when my doorbell rang. I was surprised because I wasn't expecting anyone and couldn't imagine who could be coming to see me. "Who is it?" I asked curiously.

"David."

I was shocked. I hadn't expected to hear from him ever again based on our last interaction.

"Just a minute." Butterflies entered my stomach along with nervousness. I quickly glanced at myself in the mirror and loosened my hair from the ponytail it was in. I took a deep breath before opening the door.

"Hey!"

"Hey, Nakia. Look, I'm sorry to just stop by. I was just hoping we could talk."

"Yes, please come in."

"Would you like something to drink?" I asked after he was seated in my living room.

"No, I'm good. Thank you."

"Okay. So, what's up?" I asked before sitting across from him.

"Nakia, I just want to apologize to you—for my behavior the last time I was here. That's not who I am. I was just very upset over my mom's accident, and I had a little too much to drink, and the alcohol brought out the worst in me. I should've never come over and disrespected you like that, and for that, I am genuinely sorry."

"I understand, and I accept your apology. We all have our moments. How is your mom?"

"She's doing better. She's out of the hospital and in a rehabilitation center. They're helping her with walking and things like that. She was really messed up in that accident. I thought I was going to lose her."

"Goodness, I'm so sorry to hear that, but I'm glad she's doing better. I can only imagine how scary that must have been."

"Yeah, it was." David sat silently at first. I could tell there was something he wanted to say. "Nakia, what's up with us? Should I just give up? I know I might have been moving a little too fast, but it was only because—because I'm in love with you."

David looked relieved that he'd gotten it off his chest. I was flabbergasted, and time stood still for a moment. I knew David had feelings for me, but I didn't know they were that strong. I also wasn't in love with him—yet. My feelings for him had been a roller coaster since we met. After my divorce I found him clingy and suffocating. Yet, when he was not around me, I found myself yearning for his company. The yearning is what I had been feeling since our last encounter. It was time I let my guard down and let him know how I felt. He was a good man, and I did not want to string him along.

"I mean, do you have any feelings for me at all? Or was it just a fling for you?"

I was flustered and nervous and took a moment to reply.

"Yes, babe. I'm feeling you. I'm just not in love with you—yet. But I do feel strongly about you, and I'm down to really give us a chance, if you're down. You are a wonderful man who has put up with a lot from me. I owe us a real chance." I exhaled, and relief came over me. I was being vulnerable. I was finally ready to be in a relationship.

The biggest smile spread across David's face. He stood up and walked over to where I was sitting. I stood up facing him, and he pulled me in for a hug followed by a passionate kiss that made time stand still. We spent the night together at my place, refamiliarizing ourselves with each other, and life almost felt like it was sane again.

CHAPTER 11

It was December, and David and I had been dating exclusively for about two months. So far, everything was going well—so well that we were actually planning a trip together for the holidays. I was super excited to get away and spend some time with him alone. I'd met his mom and several other family members, and I instantly fell in love with them. My life was on the up and up.

It's funny how life can feel like a movie at times, especially when all the twists and turns that we think would only happen in a movie, happen in real life. But for once there were no surprising twists or turns—just what seemed like a smooth road ahead—and things were going absolutely perfectly. I mean, almost too perfectly. I still hadn't heard from Toni, and while it bothered me, I knew it was best to give her space and let her contact me on her terms. I could only imagine how she was feeling, but I had faith that things would fall back into place with us. Eventually.

One Sunday evening, as David and I were driving back to his place after doing some shopping for our trip, we passed by a horrible accident. As we neared an intersection not far from our complex, we could see flashing lights up ahead. To top it off, the weather was terrible, and according to the weather report, we were in for a winter storm that night. As we got closer to the intersection, we realized the road was blocked. We could also see an ambulance alongside the police cars, and a little bit further down the road were two completely totaled cars. As we were waiting for an opportunity to pass through, a bloodcurdling scream echoed through the air.

The scream was so loud and so filled with emotion that it sent a chill down my spine. When I turned toward the direction of the scream, I could see a woman being held back by police officers as someone was being rolled away on a stretcher. The sheet was over the head of whoever was being rolled away, and I could only assume that the person was deceased. My heart sank as I realized that was likely the reason the woman was screaming. David let out a hesitant sigh, and I could tell he had come to the same conclusion as I had. I placed my hand on his as I knew his own mother's accident entered his mind.

After about twenty minutes of waiting, we were allowed to pass through the intersection. As David continued down the long dark road that led to our complex, we both were silent. The snow was falling heavier and faster, and I was just anxious to get home. I also was feeling kind of shook by what we had witnessed. I couldn't imagine what that woman was feeling right now. I wondered if it was her significant other being rolled away on that stretcher. Then, I wondered how I would feel if it was David being rolled away. And that's the moment that I knew— I was in love with him. Witnessing the aftermath of that horrible accident made me realize that David made me happy in ways no one else had since Jerell, and I couldn't imagine my life without him. I also realized that tomorrow, or even the next moment, wasn't promised, and I needed to let him know how I felt.

"David?"

"Yes, babe?" he replied, glancing back and forth between me and the road.

I rubbed my hand gently across his. "I love you," I said, smiling.

The biggest smile spread across his face. He lifted my hand and softly kissed it. "I love you too, babe, with all my heart."

It felt good to be in love, and I couldn't think of any better person to be in love with. My life was finally where I wanted it to be, and I was excited about what was yet to come for us. Would I be a married woman again? I hoped so.

We entered David's house to discover the electricity had gone out.

"Shit. I hope it comes back on soon."

"Why? Let me find out you're scared of the dark, Nakia."

"No, I'm not scared of the dark." I laughed. "I just know that if the heat doesn't come back on soon, we're going to freeze tonight."

"Nah, I think we'll be fine."

"Oh, yeah? How so?"

"Because I know what to do to keep both of us warm."

"Oh, really?" I giggled.

Suddenly, a small light appeared in the darkness. David had located a flashlight.

"Should we head to my bedroom? I think it'll be a lot warmer in there, to be honest," he said slyly.

Even without fully seeing his face, I knew David was grinning. "Sure. I think blankets would feel nice right about now."

"Oh, blankets aren't the only thing able to keep you warm."

"Is that right? And what else is able to keep me warm?" I asked teasingly as we headed toward David's bedroom.

"I can show you better than I can tell you."

David and I weren't cold at all that night. If anything, things might have gotten a little too spicy, because the condom broke, and we didn't notice until after we were done. But I wasn't worried. If I was pregnant, then it was meant to be, and I was sure David would be a great father.

As I laid in David's arms that night, I thought about all the possibilities that were in store for us. What if I was pregnant? What would our child be like? Who would they look like? Would I be a good mom? Would parenthood ruin our relationship like I'd seen it do to so many other couples? So many questions were running through my head, but for once, I wasn't thinking of an escape plan. Instead, I was willing to stick it out through whatever was in store for us, and I refused to let fear and anxiety chase me away from him. For the first time in a long time, I was with someone for the long run, and it felt good.

CHAPTER 12

It was a week before Christmas, and David and I had just arrived at my parents' house for a Christmas dinner since he and I would be away on Christmas day. It was also the first time he would be meeting my parents, and he was a little nervous.

"Now you know how I felt when you tried to spring me on your mom that time."

David sighed. "How did I know you would bring that up?"

"Because you know you were wrong as hell," I said, laughing. "Boy, get up out of this car, and let's go inside. There's nothing to be worried about. My parents will love you."

"Okay," David said as he got out of the car. I could tell he was still nervous though.

"Mom? Dad?" I yelled as we entered the house.

As usual, my mother had the house decorated in Christmas attire to a T. The sweet smell of mint filled the air, and I could smell an array of deliciousness wafting from the kitchen through my nostrils.

"Hey, baby," my dad said as he descended the stairs. I glanced over at David who looked like a deer caught in head-lights. Sweat had formed across his brow. I'd never seen him look so nervous.

After giving me a hug and kiss, my father walked over to David.

"Young man, it's nice to finally meet you. I've heard a lot about you."

"It's nice to meet you as well, sir," David replied before shaking my father's hand.

"Where's Mom at, Dad?"

"Oh, she's in the kitchen. She's probably in there running her mouth on that phone."

As if on cue, my mom appeared in the entryway to the living room where David and I were sitting.

"Hey, baby!" my mother greeted me in the living room. "You're early."

"Yeah, we left early because we thought we'd run into way more traffic than we did. Do you need help with anything?"

"No, baby, I'm good. Go take David into the family room for now. The food will be done shortly."

"Okay, Mom," I said before escorting David to the family room.

As we sat in the family room and talked with my dad, David was a bit shy at first. But my father, being the easygoing man he was, made sure he loosened up in no time. Soon, David and my dad were in the living room laughing and talking sports like they'd known each other for years. I was so happy they hit it off. David was the first man who my family had met since Kyle, and neither one of them cared for Kyle too much. However, I could tell by how both of them interacted with David throughout the night that he had their blessing.

After dinner and a delicious dessert, David and I said goodbye to my parents and then prepared to head back to Maryland. We'd decided not to stay the night because David had some loose ends to tie up with his business, and I had some errands to run back home before we left for our much-needed trip to the Bahamas in the upcoming week. As soon as we got in the door, we both hit the sack, exhausted from the ride home. We were both so tired that we would've overslept, had it not been for my phone ringing at 7 the next morning.

"Hello?"

"Hello, Nakia? It's Jerell."

"Ummm, hold on a for a second." I glanced over at David to make sure he was still asleep before slipping out of the bed and taking the call in the next room. "Hey, Jerell. What's going on?" I was surprised to hear from him. I could think of no reason he'd have to call me so early in the morning.

"Hey, Nakia. I'm sorry if I woke you. I'm just in a crazy situation right now, and I needed someone who was removed from the situation to give me their opinion."

"Okay."

"It's about my girlfriend. Well, she just had a baby, and I don't think it's mine."

I was shocked. While I knew Jordyn was due soon, I could've sworn she still had a month or so left in her pregnancy.

"Oh, wow, Jerell. I don't know what to say. Why don't you think the baby is yours?"

I could hear Jerell take in a breath. "Well, besides the fact that I just have a weird feeling he isn't, the baby looks nothing like me. In fact, the baby looks white!"

I wasn't surprised. The last time we'd spoken, Jordyn was pretty sure the baby was Brad's. Since I had no right to tell Jordyn's secret, I'd kept that information to myself and prayed that Jordyn would just do the right thing and tell Jerell. However, based on Jerell's phone call, she never had.

As Jerell vented to me about his situation, I simply listened. I knew David would be up soon, and I wasn't interested in explaining to him who I was talking to so early in the morning. Finally, Jerell stopped talking, and I was able to get a word in.

"Jerell, I'm so sorry you're going through this. I don't know. I guess maybe you should tell your girlfriend how you feel and see what her response is. If she truly loves you, no matter how bad it is, she'll tell you the truth." "Yeah, you're right. I'm going to give her some time to heal though. She had a C-section, and she's not feeling so well right now. But you're right. We need to talk about this before it ruins our relationship. You know, even if the baby isn't mine, I still want to be in his life, and I still love my girl. You know I have always wanted to be a father. It might be in a different form, but this is what I have always asked for."

"I'm glad to hear it, Jerell. I hope everything works out for you two, and congrats on the baby." I was convinced the reality of the situation had not kicked in yet. No man in his right mind would want to take care of another man's child. I don't care how bad he wanted to be a father.

"Thank you, Nakia."

"Well, I have to get going. I have a busy day ahead of me, but keep in touch, and let me know how things work out."

"I will. Thanks again for listening to me. I appreciate it."

"You're welcome, Jerell. Goodbye."

"Bye, Nakia."

Later that day I got a phone call from Jordyn telling me the baby had arrived. I pretended to be surprised and congratulated her on a safe and healthy delivery. Then I let her know I'd be over to see her and the baby after I returned from my trip. However, I knew at some point I'd have to let Jordyn know that Jerell was my ex, as well as let Jerell know that Jordyn and I were co-workers and friends. But, for the time being, I pushed it aside. All I was focused on was David and the Bahamas.

It was the day of our flight to the Bahamas, and David and I had arrived at the airport early. We were sitting in the waiting area waiting to board when David decided he'd head off to the bookstore and grab a magazine for the flight. While I waited for him to return, my cell phone rang. To my surprise, it was Toni.

"Hello?"

"Hi, Nakia."

There was a short awkward silence as if Toni didn't know what to say, so I spoke instead. "Hey, Toni. I'm so happy to hear from you. How have you been?"

"I've been okay—" Toni sounded as if she were about to cry, and I knew if she cried, I was going to cry too. "I'm so sorry,

Nakia. I should have never talked to you that way. You didn't do anything wrong. I was just so upset that what I thought was the perfect relationship was all a lie. I felt like a failure. I never believed Amir over you. I only took it out on you because you were the one there at the time. Then, by the time I realized I was wrong, I was too embarrassed to call you and apologize. I'm so sorry."

"It's okay, Toni. I was never angry with you. To be honest, the only reason I didn't call you is because I wanted to give you time to work through what you were going through, and I also didn't want to upset you more."

"I know. You're a good friend. Let's promise to never argue or fight again. These past couple of months without you have been awful."

"Okay, I promise. Besides, I don't know too many people who could live without me. I mean, c'mon, Toni. You know I'm amazing...."

"Whatever, chick. Let's not push it," Toni replied. We both laughed.

Toni didn't mention anything about the current status of her and Amir, and I didn't want to bombard her with questions so soon into our rekindled friendship. So instead, we chatted about how I was doing, and I let her know about things with David and me. Mid-conversation, I noticed that David had left his phone behind on the seat next to me, and the alerts were going off.

"Hey, Toni. It's almost time for our flight to start boarding. I'll call you when we return, okay?"

"Okay, girl. Have fun, and Merry Christmas!"

"Merry Christmas to you too, Toni. I'll talk to you soon."

After hanging up with Toni, I checked to make sure David was nowhere around. Then I quickly picked up his phone to take a quick look. There were a few unread text messages. A few were from his mom telling him to have a good trip and to call her when we landed so she knew we arrived safely. But there was another one from an "Unknown" phone number that caught my eye.

Either you tell her, or I will. You will not get to live out your happy ending if I don't get to live out mine. Live in your truth boo.

I quickly marked the message as unread, then exited to the home screen before putting David's phone back down on the seat next to me. My heart was pounding, and lightheadedness was setting in. What had I just read? Who was the "Unknown" sender, and what were they talking about? I hated the way I felt and wished I'd never picked up his phone. As I thought about how I could mention the text to him without looking like a nosy girlfriend, I saw him walking toward me.

"Hey, I was going to call you to ask if you wanted me to bring you anything back, but then I realized that I'd left my phone on the seat. So instead of coming back empty-handed, I got you a few magazines to read on the plane."

"Thanks, babe. That was thoughtful of you." As much as I wanted to bring up the text message, I wanted to go on my trip even more, so, I decided to keep quiet. Maybe I'd misread or misunderstood the message. Maybe it was the wrong number and the message wasn't even for him. I really needed it to be a wrong number. Everything had been going so great between us, and I really didn't want to have to deal with any drama. But, as much as I tried to ignore it and think positive, my inner voice was not trying to let me have any peace. *Girl, you know what you read. Don't doubt yourself. Something is wrong, and you need to find out what it is.*

A few minutes later, David and were seated in first class. As I prepared to turn my phone off for the plane ride, I noticed I had an unread message, and it was from an "Unknown" number as well! When I opened the message and read it, my mouth dropped open in awe.

Do you really know the man you're with?
Do you really know who David is?
You better be careful, Nakia.

AFTERWORD

As I stared down at the two bright pink lines on the white stick in my hand, I was in shock. Was I really pregnant? The thought of having a baby only brought me back to my last pregnancy experience, and the thought made me so upset, I began to hyperventilate. I was in the hotel bathroom of our suite in the Bahamas, and after a rough first day on the island filled with nausea followed by vomiting, I knew something was wrong. So, while David was on the beach, I lied and told him I was tired, then snuck away and bought a pregnancy test. Now, I had to figure out how I was going to tell him the news.

To be honest, I'd been a little uneasy ever since I'd seen the text messages from that "Unknown" sender on both of our phones, and I hadn't worked up the nerve to ask David about them. I'm sure he had to have read the message he'd received by now, but if he did, he showed no indication of it in his behavior. I was conflicted, to say the least. I'd dreamed about starting a family with David—that was, until I saw those messages. But now that I was actually pregnant, the reality of it was hitting me differently.

After calming myself, I decided I was early enough in the pregnancy to keep it a secret for a while. As much as I wanted to tell David the news, something inside me told me not to say anything to him about it right away. So, I wrapped the remnants of the test in some tissue and then tossed it in the hallway trash receptacle. I quickly changed into a swimsuit and pushed myself to join David on the beach.

As I walked along the sand, scanning the crowd and trying to find David, I thought I caught a glimpse of him up ahead, and he wasn't alone. A tall, dark-skinned man with a muscular physique was talking to David and smiling as they stood face to face, less than an inch away from each other. It looked strange, but I couldn't quite place why. Suddenly, David looked up and saw me looking at them. He seemed startled, and he quickly said something to the man, then rushed toward me.

"Who was that?"

"Oh, he's a surf instructor. I—I was asking about the lessons he offered, and he was explaining about the different levels of training he provided and what not. But I see you're feeling better. I'm glad you're up and about. What do you want to do?"

"Oh, I'm just going to take it easy and lie in the sun for a little while. You go have fun. I'll be right here."

"Oh, okay. You sure? I don't mind hanging out with you. After all, this is our vacation."

"No, I'm fine. I'll be right here. Go—get in the ocean. It's all you've been talking about."

"Okay, babe. I'll be back in a bit," he said before kissing me on the lips and heading toward the water.

As he walked off, I noticed the man that he had been talking to was staring at him funny. I couldn't quite place it, but something was wrong. All I knew was things seemed strange with David, and I needed to figure out what was going on.

THANK YOU

Thank you for reading *The Single Life*. If you enjoyed it, please take a moment to leave a review on Amazon, Barnes and Noble, Goodreads, or your preferred online retailer.

Reviews are the best way to show your support for an author and to help new readers discover their books.

ABOUT THE AUTHOR

Born in Nyack, NY and later raised in Lynchburg, VA, Marquita B. has an entrepreneurial spirit with a passion for writing. She is also the proud founder of Corks and Coils Publishing. After obtaining her Master's degree, she moved to the DC area where she enjoys spending time with her husband  and daughter. She currently works as a Product Manager for an insurance company in addition to being an author. Marquita's hobbies include singing, cooking, watching reality TV, searching for hair care products, wine tasting, and shopping.

www.ingramcontent.com/pod-product-compliance
Lightning Source LLC
Chambersburg PA
CBHW070331130626
46556CB00007B/2805